The Era of Lanterns
and Bells

Ann Tinkham

First Edition

Published by Napili Press

ISBN: 978-0-9990157-0-4 (Paperback)

ISBN: 978-0-9990157-3-5 (eBook)

Cover Design: Jessica Bell

Visit the author website at www.anntinkham.com

Contents

Tunnel Vision

It was the eyes that Lenny couldn't shake—the look in her eyes before she jumped that led to a daily nightcap of Xanax and Bourbon. When it wore off, Lenny awoke with a pounding heart to dark, watery eyes asking for help when it was already too late. That was the kicker—the eyes pleading for help when they knew it was all over. Lenny respected people who left without a trace. But the jumpers left a trace in the minds of drivers like Lenny.

In the subway business, they called subway jumping a PUT incident. Person under train. Lenny thought the term was too neat for what actually occurred. Person under train sounded as if a person were merely—oops—stuck under the train, like a pant leg or an overcoat, or even a briefcase or an umbrella. Excuse me, sir, can you please move your train off my foot? That's what a PUT incident sounded like to Lenny. If it were up to him, it would be called a GSOT. Guts splattered over tracks. In his sleep-deprived stupor after his PUT incident, he thought about proposing a name change during a weekly transit meeting, but he bit his tongue for fear of losing his job.

The guys talked, and everyone knew management put drivers under watch after a PUT incident. If the driver seemed to have some screws loose, the management team forced him to take temporary unpaid leave, which often led to permanent unpaid leave (aka termination). Lenny thought about the unfairness of the double whammy. First, he had to watch as some hard-luck case jumped in front of his train. Then he had to pretend that nothing happened for fear of management "expressing concern."

Lenny had heard from the guys that the late night/early morning shifts had the highest rates of PUTs. But as a newbie, he had no choice but to drive those shifts. His buddy Cal told him that early Monday morning was the worst. Folks dreaded the workweek ahead and saw no way out.

Lenny understood that feeling, but never saw jumping into an oncoming train as the solution.

After it happened, the Metro Area Transit or MAT, psychiatrist told him it was normal for PUT victims to experience an acute psycho-physiological reaction three weeks after the event, with elevated prolactin and increased sleep disturbance. He said that acute reactions were transitory and not correlated with the need for long-term sick leave, which was predicted independently by a high plasma cortisol level and a high depression score. Lenny didn't really catch what should be happening to him other than the sleep problems. The shrink told him he was suffering from PUT-related PTSD. The letters sounded too tidy for what he felt like inside. He felt like a train had run over him.

The reason he was sent to the MAT psychiatrist was that after the incident, his trains were running twenty minutes late. His boss pulled him into a closed-door meeting in a hot office smelling of stale coffee and told him it just wouldn't do. He sat on the edge of his desk with his arms crossed and said, "If you can't run on time, we'll have to reassign you."

The thing was, although Lenny wouldn't say this to his boss, he now had the feeling everyone on the platform was getting ready to jump. So, he kept watch over people on the platform—imagining that the punk girl, the Rastafarian, the bent-over old man, the teen in black leather were each about to jump. He pulled the brake each time he anticipated a jump. But rather than telling his boss he was busy saving lives, Lenny said, "I'll run on time, sir."

He was the last person to see her alive, and now he carried a part of her with him wherever he went. The worst part was that he lost a part of himself when she jumped and couldn't get it back. Her eyes asked for help, for him to stop the train and save her. But he couldn't.

"Go back to sleep, Lenny. Please go back to sleep," his wife would say when she looked over and saw his shining eyes in the darkness.

"I could have helped if I had known. I just didn't know."

"It's not your fault. Now close your eyes." He tried, but the jumper's eyes prevented him from closing his.

"It's not fair," Lenny said.

"No, it's not. But going over and over it will not change it. Did you ever think that perhaps she wanted to go? Who knows? Maybe you did her a favor. What if she had terminal cancer or lost everything she had in the world? Maybe she was a criminal on the run."

"She wasn't a criminal."

"How do you know? You didn't know her from Eve."

"I could tell by her eyes."

"Oh, Len, please."

The jumper's eyes locked onto his, and then she leapt. It was 3:03 a.m. when Lenny cranked the brakes and screamed into the intercom. "Woman Under! Woman Under!" Had he known she was going to jump, he could've stopped the train in time.

Later Lenny was reprimanded by his supervisor, "The code for 'Man'—not 'Woman'—'Under' is 12-9. You don't

say 'Man Under' when someone is down for the count."
Lenny felt he was lucky to have produced some words—any
words, let alone remember some ridiculous code meaning
someone was being run over by a train.

"I'll remember next time," Lenny promised.

"She would still be alive," he said to his coworkers before the
weekly meeting. Four drivers huddled at a small wobbly card
table with vintage trash-heap-chic metal folding chairs,
appropriate furnishings for barely-lit dank subterranean
offices that smelled of fuel, earth, and mildew. Two guys had
flipped the chairs so the back was in the front and the other
pair with the back in the back. One duo straddled and the
other slumped.

"Yeah, and then she'd find another train to finish the
job," said a seasoned driver with a mouthful of jelly donut.
He clearly eschewed the chewing-with-his mouth-closed
lesson. "Forget about it, Lenny."

"How can you tell? I mean what are the signs that
someone is about to jump? Can you tell by looking at their
eyes?" asked Lenny, his bloodshot eyes pleading for an
answer.

"Who knows? If people want to die, they'll find a way.
You can't analyze every person on the platform at warp

speed. It will drive you nuts; then you'll end up a jumper—like the driver a few years back who couldn't take it anymore and jumped. Can you imagine doing that to one of us? I mean, hell, you can OD, shoot or gas yourself, call that Keborkan dude," said a driver who looked part heavy-weight and part couch potato, devouring a glazed donut in two motions—in and down his gullet. "You know…if you wanna do it," his words barely intelligible with the donut taking up all his linguistic real estate.

"The name's Kevorkian. He's dead," said a petite man with a fussy goatee nibbling on a sprinkled donut, sounding a bit too up on Kevorkian's comings and goings for a man who wanted to live. He wiped his closely trimmed beard with a folded napkin after every bite. Still he had sprinkles adorning his goatee.

"Whatever. I'm sure there are Kevorkian types out there who will help you if the price is right. Anyway, why people choose the subway, I'll never understand. Why make a driver do your job for you? Be a man about it. Hear what I'm sayin'?" said the glazed donut guy stuffing donut number three into his mouth and chasing it with the infamous Transit sludge. Months earlier an anonymous employee had posted a sign by the coffee machine: DRINK AT YOUR OWN RISK, which was swiftly removed by management. The brief witch-hunt for the coffee bandit left management empty-handed. They threatened to pull the coffee service, which they reminded everyone was an employee perk after all. The drivers joked about a coffee lawsuit, not from scalding coffee burning their laps but from coffee so bad it was lethal.

The guys nodded and shook their heads in disgust at cowardly jumpers making drivers do their dirty work. Lenny's head was frozen stiff, like the rest of his body—rigor without the mortis. He stared at the Driver Appreciation bulletin board affixed in the space next to the card table along with yellowing OSHA placards and Transit rules and regs. Someone had squashed a juicy spider on the bloodborne pathogens section and no one, not even the janitorial staff, had ever bothered to wipe it off. The spider illustrated the cautionary text that had gone unread.

Lenny blinked to wash away the tears forming and not cooperating with his cease and desist order to his tear ducts. His lip was anything but stiff now; it was starting to twitch and tremble.

He was known among the guys as the donut scarfing dude, usually polishing off four or five donuts at the weekly Transit meeting, but today the boxes of bear claws, jelly donuts, glazed donuts, cinnamon buns, and Danishes turned his stomach.

"Len," Cal said offering him a bear claw in their weekly ritual. Cal played the part of the donut-eating contest assistant.

"Not hungry," Lenny said holding up his palm in a stopping donut traffic gesture.

Cal shot him a "what the fuck" glance and jammed the entire pastry in his mouth for a cheap laugh.

Lenny pushed out an unconvincing laugh that sounded more like a moan, shook his head, and shuffled toward the clustered meeting chairs. Staff and management alike never bothered to line them up unless the Transit Authority head honcho was making a rare appearance to put a positive spin on reorganization and headcount reduction.

The regional director of the Transit Authority kicked off the meeting. "We've got a lot to cover, so I'll do Q&A at the end. You all have undoubtedly heard that we had another PUT incident on the green line at South Street. Lenny here was the operator. That's thirty-four this year and we haven't even made it through the holidays. Jesus. Usually have several that celebrate Hanukah, Christmas, and the New Year with a leap." The dozens of drivers changed positions in their stiff chairs and sighed, muttered, and cleared their throats. Lenny felt as if he might have to make a speedy exit so the other guys wouldn't see him if he broke up.

"The Commission suggests soothing music for suicide prevention. They say it works on animals. Not sure how they've tested that one. Elevator music in chicken coops? Mozart in pig pens." The meeting attendees chuckled between donut bites and coffee gulps. "The Commission is open to suggestions. If you have an idea, drop it into the anonymous suggestion box on your way out. They're also talking about putting up safety fences. It would be like a subterranean barnyard down here."

Everyone laughed but Lenny. All the other guys could take it; why couldn't he? He wondered how he could keep working there if the PUTs were such a common occurrence. Perhaps he could if he could somehow prevent this from happening again.

He supposed he should feel lucky. Some guys were cursed. One driver had twenty-three man unders; another eighteen; still another five. Eighteen told him, "You get used to it after a while. My first three were the hardest. After that, I figured I did them a favor." Twenty-three nodded and picked his teeth with a toothpick. He added, "Don't take this the wrong way, but after you've had enough of them, they're like bugs on a windshield. Nothing a little wiper fluid can't take care of." Five said under his breath so that only Lenny could hear, "I'm going to look into another line of work. One that

9

doesn't involve enclosed spaces, speeding trains, and suicides."

Lenny pictured the subway walls closing in on him, the entrapment Five described, the platform filled with jumpers, and his mandate to run on time. He was the conductor of a high-speed murder weapon. His chest cavity compressed, as though it could no longer house his beating, bleeding heart. He had to do something, anything that would alleviate the situation. He was compelled to put a recommendation in the suggestion box so that no one would have to experience what he was going through. He jotted his idea down on a napkin, careful not to show it to anyone. Cal elbowed him to sneak a peek and played at swiping it from him, but Lenny quickly stuffed it in his pocket. On his way out, he dropped it into the tight slot of the suggestion box.

Several weeks after the meeting in which Lenny contributed to the suggestion box, he and his lunch box and thermos were cornered by members of the MAT management team who called him into the conference room. The lanky member of the team, known for his impatient surliness, held up the suggestion and asked if it was Lenny's.

Lenny leaned in to make sure.

"Yes, sir, it is." A jolt of anxiety ricocheted from Lenny's heart to his hands. He shoved them into his pockets to obscure his trembling fingers. *Why were they following up with him? How did they know the suggestion was his, given that the suggestion box was anonymous? Did they decode the handwriting? Did they have someone watching him?* Then it struck him that they might ask him to elaborate on his suggestion—give them ideas for making it happen. With his contribution, he was now being sought out by the management team. He might be rewarded for making the best of a bad situation.

"Lenny, we're going to have to ask you to take a leave of absence."

"What? Why?" Lenny's heart beat wildly. "I thought this was an anonymous suggestion box."

"We have no choice but to intervene for legal reasons. Plus, we don't want this or your attitude problem permeating our team and spreading to other drivers."

Shame washed over Lenny; they knew he didn't cut the mustard.

"Okay." Lenny and his lunch box started to walk out. Then he turned around and said, "Could I please have my suggestion back?"

"Certainly." The manager handed Lenny his slip of paper. As he walked out, he reread his words: *We need to provide free bags on the platforms to cover jumpers' eyes*

11

Two Strings Short

I t was one of those days. Ominous signs of the future were springing up at every print journal outlet, including mine, the *Los Angeles Times*. The most striking example was *The New York Times* trying every tactic to stay afloat—even running controversial, poorly researched *Enquirer*-type stories. I was a shipmate on a grand fleet of ships that was sinking slowly. Bit by bit, the newspaper business was being dismantled. All the things we had taken for granted for decades were being undone in a matter of years by the new kid on the block—Internet news and blogs. Otherwise known as blah-ughs by yours truly. We were approaching a new era—the era of the rant-as-publishable piece. Journalism's reality TV equivalent. And the kicker was, I had to keep my disgruntledness to myself.

First, you had the carbon footprint Nazis—mostly twenty- and thirty-somethings—who were giddy about the demise of the newspaper. Their vision—to eliminate all printed news by 2020—would allegedly save the Brazilian rainforest. I didn't want to rain on their tropical parade by telling them the extinction of the printed newspaper might save a Toucan or two, but the spread of beef farms for fast-food burgers would not. However, if one displayed any indication of carbon footprint opposition, the green brigade moved in for a stamp-out-global-warming preach-a-thon.

Second, you had management trolling for disgruntled curmudgeonly types (that would be me, but I'm a stealth guy) who weren't "embracing change" or being "virtual thought leaders." The top dogs ambushed the resisters in the cubicle labyrinth with the dreaded pink slip. After participating in a perky three-day webinar, "Championing Change," during which we all gained the title "Change Champions," with T-shirts and baseball caps to match, I wanted to tell management to put change where the sun don't shine.

That afternoon, I took the long way home from the *Los Angeles Times* to work on my beer gut and pasty complexion but mostly to spare my wife and girls my black mood du jour. It emerged so often, my wife called me the "Monster That Doesn't Mean It" to help Sadie, five, and Chelsea, eight, deal with me. Chelsea was old enough to counter with, "Mom, it's not a monster; it's just Dad needing a time-out."

Time out, not necessarily. Time travel, definitely. Back to the days when newspaper journalists mattered.

As a crew member of a failing enterprise, I was so cranky and incorrigible at home, I'm surprised my wife stuck around. With my edgy, irritable ways, I half-expected to come home one night to an empty house and a note—*Dear Ben: Took the girls, the dog, but left the parrot. Figured you could use some company— even if it's only squawking. What a pair you'll be—the squawker and the kvetcher.*

My wife had tried everything including countless flavors of religion to bring back the Ben she married. She talked so incessantly and with longing about the Ben she married, it felt like she was having an affair with the guy. I wanted to clock him one, and had to constantly remind myself the guy was me. In another time. When I still mattered. In my bereft state, I boldly declared there was no proof of the divine, not in man-made artifacts, natural wonders, especially not in everyday life.

One day after my triple-shot espresso that verged on a quad-shot order, but my barista intervened, I meandered through downtown Los Angeles, my thoughts devoted to clever money-making schemes to keep the newspaper, in its print format, alive—ruminations that had become a daily practice. I am ashamed to say I couldn't think of anything better than do-it-yourself ego columns. People would pay the newspaper a nominal fee to run columns about themselves. Or a contest for reducing one's carbon footprint. The winner would receive a donated Prius, a personal wind turbine, a solar razor, or other eco-friendly gadget. Hell, even a solar vibrator. With ideas like these, the newspaper would surely fold long before my retirement. Good thing I wrote a personal interest column and wasn't in charge of business development.

As I walked through the tunnel, bland and blasé, my ears—anxious to take a break from my down-in-the-dumps brain—detected the sound of music. My brain and ears played tug-o-war, but my ears won; a black man about my age was playing a melodious, waltzing violin. Despite the beautiful sound emanating from the strings, something wasn't quite right. I stopped and studied the violinist for several minutes and finally discerned that he was playing a violin with only two strings. Imagine what he could do with four!

He was a raggedy black man in subterranean concert wear with slick black hair parted neatly on the left side. His clothes were tattered, wrinkled, and stained, but he wore a bowtie clipped beneath his chin. The hand that held the bow was bound by rags wrapped tightly to his knuckles.

After he finished his piece, I applauded, pulled out a five-dollar bill and offered it to him. He wouldn't make eye contact. Then with the bow, he directed me to drop the five into his hat on the sidewalk. I obliged. I noticed his hat was empty except for my crumpled bill.

"It was lovely, but why do you only have two strings?" I inquired. He mumbled and grumbled and was restless in my presence, pacing back and forth in front of an overflowing shopping cart with the words "Little Disney Concert Hall" scrawled on the side. The violinist looked like he might pack up because of me, but he started playing again, probably to get me to stop talking. His tactic worked. Eventually I strolled out of the tunnel a little lighter than when I entered. The music—his music—had lifted me out of my doom and gloom and into the world of lightness. Grace in grittiness.

I couldn't stop thinking about the violinist who was two strings short of a complete violin. As I worked on my column, commuted, spent time with my family, I found my thoughts turning to the raggedy man. He was an unfinished story. And as a writer, I felt compelled to finish it.

Each time I returned to the tunnel, the violinist was so immersed in his playing, he would hardly notice me. The second time, I said, "It's beautiful." And he said, "Just listen and shut your trap. You hear?"

The third time, I inquired about his missing strings and he said, "They just snapped off. Why you so nosey, Mister?

Don't you have some place to go like regular folks?" I wanted to say, *No, actually I don't. I'm on the verge of extinction. And like all on the endangered species list, I'm desperate.*

The fourth time I asked him where he learned to play like that, he said, "Julliard."

I chuckled to myself and said, "*The* Julliard?"

He said, "Yep. That's the one."

"What's your name?"

"What's it to you, Mister?"

"I'm a journalist and I like to make note of talented musicians. Who knows, maybe I'll write about you in my column."

He seemed to like that answer and proudly said, "Alright, then. Everett D. Washington. The D's for Dwight."

"Everett D. Washington, it's an honor to hear you play. I just wish you had a full set of strings."

He laughed for the first time since I'd met him. "If you feel that way, imagine how I feel."

Astonished, I rushed to call Julliard the next morning to inquire about Everett D. Washington. I calculated his years of attendance by his probable age—the late sixties.

"Nope, sir, no one in our files by that name," said a downbeat girl in the records department. "Anything else I can help you with?"

"Listen, if you happen to come across Everett D. Washington, call me at 818-783-9873. Okay?" I said, thinking I was sounding desperate.

The records girl snorted and said, "I already told you there's no one in our records with that name."

My heart sank. I wanted to believe I had discovered a street virtuoso, but it seemed he was mentally ill and delusional.

I visited the tunnel again that afternoon and found Everett scrawling names on the sidewalk—Samuel, Jackie, Betty, Arnie, and Jonathan.

"Who are those people?" I asked.

"My classmates at Julliard," he responded without hesitation.

Right, his imaginary friends. I was saddened by Everett, his imaginary friends, and his shopping cart filled with bottles, cans, soiled blankets, plastic toys, discarded tools, and, on top, his violin case.

"Will you play me a tune today?"

"No, Mister, can't you see I'm busy?"

"Maybe next time, then," I said, hoping to hear him tickle his strings. Everett made no promises.

When I got home, my wife said I had received a call from Julliard. "Planning to go back to school in the performing arts, sweetie?" she teased me. "Let's see, you have two left feet, sing like a cat in heat, and can't keep the beat. So, will it be acting, then?"

I had heard all these things before, but not as a coherent litany of my failings in the performing arts. I must say it did smart a bit. As a writer, I'd always hidden behind my words— tinkering with turns of phrases—but sometimes I imagined a more colorful existence as a stage performer.

"Yes, a postmodernist, my dear."

"There's a message for you. I didn't listen to the whole thing," she said as she prepared tacos, the beans smelling of cumin and cayenne.

I walked into the office to retrieve my messages. "Mr. Jaspers, you called inquiring about an Everett D. Washington. Our records show that he attended Julliard from 1967 to '69. Our records indicate that he never completed his studies."

I don't know why exactly, but I was elated. I had every reason to believe that the violinist in the tunnel was Everett D. Washington, former Julliard student. But now I had to figure out what a virtuoso was doing in a forgotten tunnel on the streets of L.A.

I began writing about Everett and his two-stringed violin in my newspaper columns. After the second column came out, calls and violin donations started rolling in. Occasionally each of us is struck by behavior that gives us renewed faith in human beings. This was one of those occasions.

A woman with a Spanish accent called to donate her son's violin. An elderly man with a shaky voice said he had Burgess violins just sitting in his basement taking up space. An upper-crusty sounding woman claimed to have purchased a violin for Everett and wondered where to drop it off.

It got to the point where I started turning people away. In just a few weeks, I had offers of a dozen violins and two cellos. It made me think, though, that such a program for people in need wouldn't be a bad idea.

My next challenge would be to approach Everett about the instruments. I had to be careful about how I did it. He appeared to be a creature of habit; he stood in the exact spot every day with his cart on his left—between himself and the tunnel wall— and his case on top of his belongings. He faced toward the west. He might turn down my offer for new instruments. The other issue was one of street people stealing from each other. If I gave Everett instruments, he might become a target. I couldn't live with myself if that happened.

When I told my wife about my plan for building trust before the instrument hand-off, she yelled, flailing dishtowel in hand, "Are you nuts? Don't you think you're taking this whole thing a little too far? So, you spend the night on skid row, get yourself killed, and then what? What do I tell the girls? 'Your father died on skid row having a sleepover with a homeless guy?'" She turned and faced the kitchen sink and furiously loaded the dishwasher, making an extra racket for dramatic effect.

"It will be fine. Really. I won't sleep. I'll just keep watch."

"You've gone and lost your marbles. When you find them, let me know—okay? I can tell you one place you won't find them—on flipping skid row."

I took that as a cautious yes.

Then I told Everett about my plan to spend the night on skid row.

"You outta your mind, Mister? You know there are cockroaches and rats and nut cases and criminals and shady characters and drug dealers and guns to name just a few of the problems? Don't get me wrong. I can make a space for you, but you aren't going to like it. I can guarantee that."

I took that as a resounding yes.

My wife was on a conversation strike to dissuade me from my skid row sleepover with Everett. Little did she know that it was a welcome relief from the mundane chatter of daily living. *Did you take out the recycling? When are we going to remodel the kitchen? What did your mother say she wanted for her birthday— foot warmers, a sweater for her dachshund, or a chip-and-dip platter? Francine wants us to ask the Beckhams when they plan to start organizing the neighborhood potluck. Why can't she ask?*

When I would forget about the strike, she stuck her palm in my face and shook her head. The girls were recruited for the strike, too, but neither could see the point nor could they refrain from teasing me about my friend, the violinist bum. Frankly, they all thought I was going off the deep end —even five-year-old Sadie.

Maybe I was.

Everett and I arranged a meeting place near skid row. He stressed the importance of going there together. If I arrived without him, I would be a walking billboard—MUG ME NOW! He gave me strict orders *not* to bring a wallet or wear a watch, belt, or expensive shoes. He gave me a wardrobe assignment. Old sweatshirt, sweatpants, and worn-out, old-school sneakers. None of the Michael Jordan Air-type basketball shoes. "They'll kill you first and then take your shoes," he said. "They don't pay no mind to life when there are valuables to be had. Do you get my drift? Also, no jeans, unless they're Levis. No one wants old school Levis. Last thing—look and act tough. You can't let 'em smell your fear, you hear? They smell it and it's all over."

We met in a deserted parking lot littered with shattered auto glass, fast food garbage, and rusty auto parts. As Everett pushed his overflowing cart toward me, he looked agitated. He was leaning over the cart with his arms covering the contents in an awkward pushing position.

"Don't know why people can't leave me be. Everyone is staring at me, wanting to steal my stuff. I think the government put them up to it. They've got operatives who are targeting me. So, I have to carefully guard my cart and hide my valuables. Otherwise people will take everything I have." Everett was scanning the vacant lot for potential operatives.

"What people?"

"All people. Maybe even you. How do I know you're not working for the government on assignment to get my stuff?" His eyes widened as he was struck with this realization. "Villains, thieves, hustlers, good-for-nothings. That's what people are, except for Beethoven, Hayden, Mozart, and other cool cats. Those guys wouldn't take my stuff; I'm sure of it."

"Do you think I'm like that—someone who steals?"

"Most likely."

"Have you seen signs of it?"

"How do I know you're not scoping out my joint so that you can steal from my crib?"

"Your crib?" I asked. Everett pointed to his cart.

"Really, you have nice stuff, but there's nothing I want. You'll just have to take my word for it." I wanted to tell him about the violins to underscore that not only was I not stealing from him, but I wanted to give him instruments as gifts. Although I was tempted, now wasn't the time. In his paranoid state, he might conjure up a conspiracy theory—that the violins were plants with bugs and every time he played, the government operatives would listen to his music, maybe even record it for sale, put it on the airwaves, like a crazy classical version of *Soul Train*, and not pay Everett a cent.

On our way to skid row, we passed many oblivious pedestrians (who would dare to venture out in such a neighborhood? Oh right, a desperate newspaperman). Everett either flashed the hairy eyeball or yelled profanities at them. I offered a half-hearted wave in apology.

Maybe this wasn't such a good idea after all. Perhaps I would have to concede to my wife and girls that I, in fact, was a tad bonkers.

By the time we arrived, the sun had nearly swooped beneath the highway, which curved above the makeshift village. The rough-and-tumble residents were lined up in a clearly-defined pecking order with temporary shelters, beds, tables, and chairs—the highest-status residents were sheltered by the highway. The stench was of smelly socks, bourbon, cigarettes, exhaust, garbage, body odor, and an outhouse— minus the house. The mood was at once somber, raucous, chaotic, and aggressive, with people milling about, trading cigarettes for booze, sharing stories from the street, guarding their territory, and pissing everywhere imaginable.

Everett continued to push his cart, with his body protecting his valuables. "Oh, no you don't, Pokey," he called out. "Skippy, watch it!" He twisted toward me in a whiplash move. "See what I mean?"

He directed his cart to an area that was directly beneath a lighted five-story apartment building.

"This is where my crib goes. Right here under the twinkling lights. See that up there? That's how Beethoven and Mozart lived—in beautiful, dazzling homes. I like it here because it makes me grateful."

"Grateful?" I asked. "Why?" His mood had shifted from agitated to serene.

"Just knowing that they graced this planet with their musical genius fills me with an unspeakable joy. Have you ever felt that, Ben?"

Unspeakable joy? Not lately. But here's this guy who has nothing but his music and two strings and he is filled with unspeakable joy. "Yes, I used to."

Everett smiled. "I'm continuing what the great masters started, so I'm part of them—one continuous composition of fluidity, lightness, and being."

It was at this point that I actually had to do a mental double take; here I was a disgruntled journalist on skid row having a conversation with a grateful homeless guy about the musical masters. It didn't compute.

"Do you want to set up camp for the night?"

I didn't really know what this meant, but I nodded.

He burrowed into his cart and pulled out a dirty flowered quilt and an old camping blanket. He held up both. "Which do you prefer? Frilly or the wilderness variety?"

I figured he preferred the latter, so I said, "Frilly."

"I knew it! I had you pegged," he exclaimed as he offered me the filthy frilly quilt.

"Why'd you peg me as frilly?" My manly side felt a little bruised. I was just deferring to my host.

"Don't get me wrong. I'm not sayin' you're a girly-man. I just think you're a little soft is all, Newspaper Man." He slapped me on the back and chuckled. "So just set them down side by side, and I'll brew us up some Folgers. You like Folgers? It's instant—all I've got."

"Folgers is great." I hated instant coffee.

"You're in luck, then." After several minutes of clanking and clamoring and rooting around in his cart, he produced a camping stove and a jar of Folgers. "Oh, hell, I don't have any water. I'll be right back—lickety split. Don't go anywhere—okay?"

Everett practically skipped off, reminding me of the Scarecrow from *The Wizard of Oz*. His hospitality was contagious—so much so that I nearly forgot where I was. But in his absence, my journalistic eyes studied a toothless, ratty-haired lady with a tuberculosis rattle of a laugh, a bulldog-looking man with a patch over his eye, and a skinny kid with hollowed-out eyes and bony cheeks who was shooting up. *Where were his parents?*

My man, Everett, was back in a flash with a big jug of water. I didn't want to know where he or one of his compadres had fetched the water from—all the options were unpalatable. If he boiled it, it should, in theory, kill all the germs and bacteria—right?

"Now, you sit back while I serve you. You won't have to lift a finger."

We sat on frilly and camouflage as the water heated to a boil, Everett spilling his knowledge about the lives of his mentors and I content to recline and soak in the incongruous ambience.

As Everett poured the gutter water into a pan, a tall man sporting a long beard twirled into two points and a black gypsy-style bandana walked up with his hand out. "Rent time, Big E."

"Oh, bug off, Wrangler." Wrangler didn't leave. He came in closer and hovered over Everett and his camping stove.

"Pay up or you're out. You know the rules."

"They're your rules. No one else's." Wrangler whipped out a switchblade and waved it in the air above Everett.

Everett turned to me and said, "Wrangler has taken it upon himself to collect rent for an area he doesn't own. King of nothing. Some of the suckers here ante up. Not me." Then to Wrangler he said, "Go ahead, slit my throat. What do I care?"

Wrangler, still holding his switchblade in the air, glared at me. "Who's this tired-looking corporate dude who's in homeless camouflage? I ain't buying it."

Not bad for a quick, on-the-spot assessment.

"He's my agent."

"What do you need an agent for? You ain't got nothin."

"My music, man. Now piss off!"

Having made no headway with Everett, he settled on me as his next victim. "I'm not leaving 'til he pays up. If you're his agent, you're responsible for him." Wrangler held his knife uncomfortably close to my chin.

"How much do you want?" I reached into my pocket where I had stashed three twenties.

"How much you got?" Wrangler asked, waving his knife toward my pocket.

"It doesn't work like that, Wrangler. If you're charging rent, it's a set fee. You don't charge it based on what another guy's got," said Everett, now pouring two cups of piping-hot Folgers into used paper cups.

"That's my system. If you don't like it, go squat on someone else's land."

"Fine, here, take forty bucks." I held out two twenties.

"Is that all you have? Pull out your pockets." At that moment, Everett threw one of the cups of scalding coffee into Wrangler's face. Wrangler dropped the knife, bent over, and grasped at his face. Everett dove for the switchblade, closed it, and calmly shoved it in his pocket.

To me, Everett said, "It's playing dirty, but you gotta do what you gotta do—right? Only problem is I wasted a good cup of coffee." He turned to Wrangler and said, "Now that's a fair trade. Don't get nothing in life for free. Your mama never teach you that? Probably not. Ain't no mama would ever claim you."

Wrangler shouted a string of obscenities in lieu of wielding a knife and ended his tirade with, "You'll be fucking sorry you messed with the Wrangler."

As Wrangler shuffled off in defeat, Everett, who was mixing his third cup of Folgers, said, "See, now, you played that ALL wrong. You played into his hand, and I had to bail you out. He got the best of you and used it to his advantage. That's the name of the game around here; try to get on top. If you show any sign of weakness, you're going down."

"I'm not used to switchblades in my face."

"Okay, I'll give you that." He sat down on the camping blanket and sipped his Folgers. "Mmm-mmm! This is what I live for. This, the greats, and my two-stringer."

I thought this was as good a time as any to bring up the four-stringers.

"So, I got this idea the other day, Everett."

"Yeah, you newspapermen are full of ideas."

"Right you are. So, what would you say if I told you I could get you not one but two new violins?

His eyes lit up above his paper cup. "You're pulling my leg—right?"

"Nope, I've got them at home waiting for you."

"Holy moly! Eight strings waiting to be played! I've gotten so used to two strings; it'll be like going from one leg to two!" A glum shadow passed over his face. "Sadly, I can't take you up on your offer, Newspaper Man."

"Why not?"

Everett held his coffee cup up in the air and moved it from the left side of skid row to the right. "This is why not. Word spreads that I have new violins, I'll be a target. They'd be wrestled away, offered up to the top dogs, then sold on the black market. And if people find out you've been holding out, you'd better get ready for a face adjustment. And I'm not talking plastic surgery."

"I've factored this in and have a plan."

"Okay, let's hear it."

We were supposed to meet in Roosevelt Park on a Friday afternoon. I sat flanked by six violin cases on display. I would let Everett have his pick of the bunch. I spot-checked my watch, and he was already an hour late. I had forgotten to factor in cart-pushing time.

I pulled out the *Los Angeles Times* to admire my column—this one was about Fatima, a female teenage suicide bomber who abandoned the mission just in time. The interview with her—through a Pakistani translator—was both riveting and frightening. She was now seeking asylum with a Pakistani family in Orange County; she would never be able to go home again. I still hadn't quite grasped what would lead a girl her age into the grips of the suicide bomb squad. I was writing a series of columns about Fatima because, no doubt, my readers were wondering the same thing.

"Something capturing your attention in the *Times*, Newspaper Man?" Everett and his cart wheeled themselves up to the bench. I should have heard him approaching—the tip-off being his cart's squeaky wheels.

"Oh, no, nothing really." I was embarrassed to be caught in the act of column admiration.

"So, what you got for me?" he asked and then scanned the cases on both sides of me. "This wasn't a setup after all, Newspaper Man. I must tell you in all honesty, I thought you might be turning me in. I almost didn't come. But the Beethoven voice inside me said, 'Everett, the strings await!' And lo and behold, he wasn't kidding! That Ludwig, man, never lets me down."

"Why would I turn you in?"

"You wouldn't be the first." Then he leaned in and said, "Even family members have turned me in!"

"There's nothing to turn you in for."

"You may be book smart, Newspaper Man, but you're not at all street smart. Consider vagrancy, for one."

"You're not a vagrant to me. You're a street performer! Okay, let's look at these, shall we?" I opened the cases, one by one. Everett's eyes sparkled like a child's scanning Christmas presents scattered beneath a bejeweled tree.

Then his eyes zeroed in on one of the violins, and he looked as though he had seen a ghost.

"What is it?" I followed his gaze to see what was wrong.

"Do you have any idea what that is?" I leaned over to look inside and saw *Stradivarius*. I had heard the name: a line of high-end violins.

"Do you like it?"

"It's exquisite."

"It's yours."

"Oh...I can't possibly...Care if I give it a whirl?" he asked leaning over and delicately pulling it out of its case. He inspected the date and said, "This is an oldie but goodie, Newspaper Man." He placed his fingers on the neck and began stroking the strings with the bow, quietly at first and then the piece erupted.

When he finished, he bowed and said, "Paganini, Concerto for Violin and Orchestra No. 2 in B minor, Opus 7, written in 1826."

As Everett played each instrument, he announced the pieces with fanfare—Wolfgang Amadeus Mozart, Violin Concerto No. 4 in D Major; Bela Bartok, Concerto for Violin and Orchestra No. 2; Felix Mendelssohn, Concerto for Violin and Orchestra in E Minor, Opus 64.

"Which ones will it be?" I asked.

Everett chose the Gobetti and Mozanni.

"But what about the Stradivarius?"

34

"Trust me. I can't take that one. I'd be a dead man walking."

"I told you that you can have any of them. What am I going to do with them? If you don't want it, I'll give it to another street musician."

Everett reached over and held my forearm. "Oh, no, you won't."

He placed the violins on top of his cart and began to wheel it carefully back from whence he came. But then he stopped abruptly. "I forgot...Where will I hide these?"

"I've set up a locker for you in Roosevelt Park's recreation center. You can lock them up for the night as long as you do it before 10:00 p.m." I gave him the location, the locker number, and the combination.

"Newspaper Man, I take back what I said about you. You aren't such a street numbskull after all." He threw his head back in glee.

Weeks later, at the urging of my wife—I owed her for the crazies of the past year—I took the Stradivarius to an auctioneer. I was never one to be bothered with converting assets to cash. I had turned down my grandfather's grandfather clock, which went to my sister and eventually sold for $50,000. My mother's antique butterfly trunk—which

was so musty and old, I thought it housed ghosts as a kid—
my brother sold for $10,000 on eBay. And now this.

The auctioneer inspected it closely, sniffed it, held it up
to the light, caressed it, and called in auctioneer
reinforcement.

"Yes, *bianca* alright—egg white, gum arabic, and honey."

Just as I was wondering how she could detect these
agents, a short man with pointed features—a bit rat-like—
went through the same routine minus the sniffing. Shouldn't
the rat-man be the sniffer? Through sniffs, harrumphs,
pursed lips, and glances, they had communicated their
assessments to each other.

A tall woman with a faux-British accent and an eyepiece
lodged in front of her left eye was the first to speak,
"Mister...What was it again?"

"Ben."

"Ben, has this been in the family for some time?"

"Uh, no."

"How did you acquire this Stradivarius, Ben?
Inheritance?"

"It's a long story."

"Oh, we have time." They all nodded. I explained the
column, the virtuoso, and the in-kind donations.

"Really?" the faux-British woman said as though she had just smelled a rat. The three auctioneers exchanged shooting glances.

"Yes, really. So, what's the verdict, guys?"

The faux-British woman appeared to have used a silencer on the other two. She spoke, this time with a stronger faux accent with a giveaway tinge of Australian. Clearly, she needed a better language coach.

"Ben," she said, appearing to ready herself for a lecture. You may not be aware that this Stradivarius is from the golden age, which spanned from 1700 to 1720. With all due respect to you, Ben, Stradivarii"—she paused for impressive plural effect—"from this age are mostly accounted for. What this means is that Stradivarii" (as if I hadn't caught the impressive pronunciation the first time) "that pop up willy-nilly may very well have been stolen. Now don't, by any means, think that I'm accusing you of being a Stradivarius thief. It's just that this is, well, very out of the ordinary, to put it mildly."

She eyed me up and down, perhaps searching for violin heist clues, but seeing only an average, pudgy, bearded middle-aged man, she called a sudden conference of the auctioneers and the Stradivarius in the back of the store.

After five minutes of unsuccessfully trying to eavesdrop, I called to the conferees, "Please, can I just get a price quote and I'll be on my way?"

The conferees and the Stradivarius glided to the front of the store. "Ben, I'm afraid we're going to have to hold onto this until we clear you."

"Clear me? For what? It was a donation, as I mentioned."

At this point, the faux-British lady lost all accents, British or otherwise, and became a straight-shooting American. "I'm not sure how to say this. But this Strad has been missing for over a century. We conferred with our records and this was owned by a New York violinist who, on his deathbed, revealed that the instrument he played for years was a Stradivarius stolen from Carnegie Hall nearly a half-century earlier. Previously, it had been stolen from a manor house in Germany during World War II and made its way across the Atlantic. Our records further show that this one was Strad's prized instruments. The German owner, Heinrich Siegfried, had purchased it in Paris in 1805. The good news is that the reward is $500,000."

"And how much is the violin worth?"

The auctioneers cast their eyes downward, deferring to the formerly demure British, now cut-to-the-chase American woman, to field this question. She breathed in as though about to launch into a soaring aria and exhaled, manicured hand on chest. "Approximate value is $5 million, give or take a couple hundred thousand."

Although not an asset man, even I was rendered speechless. I had been displaying on a park bench, flinging into and out of my Honda, carting around in my car—next to my hamburgers, French fries, and soda—a $5 million violin.

Wood from spruce, willow, and maple trees shaped into a violin, covered with egg white and honey.

And now this artifact worth millions.

No sooner than my brain had processed the figure—tripping over zeros—I was onto the more interesting question: what made humans assign value to artifacts made of simple raw materials throughout history? And what was it about the Stradivarius that was, according to the human mind, worth millions of dollars? Humans—exceedingly flawed—were occasionally capable of prodigious perfection.

Of course, the tree huggers would have objected to the exploitation of trees for any purpose, even a higher purpose like music. With them in charge, there would be no such artifact, just electronica reproducing orchestral sounds on computers.

Perhaps the Stradivarius was proof of the divine.

I would never admit this to anyone, but receiving the reward money was a burden to me. My original vision (which, thankfully, I didn't share with my wife) was to give the money to Everett to upgrade his existence. I had this idea that I would take the reward money and set up Everett in an apartment close to his favorite tunnel. Maybe I could even talk him into playing with a city orchestra instead of in a tunnel.

I explained my ideas to Everett one day while he was taking a break from playing his four-stringer. But Everett made it clear that, aside from upgrading from two to four strings, he wasn't the least bit interested in a new and improved life. He insisted that he had been around the block—in fact was never off the block—and had narrowed his life down to the essentials—music, air, and sustenance—in that order. When he put it like that, it was enticing to subscribe to such a simple life formula.

Everett said, "Listen, I don't want to live like you so-called normal people do…I like my life just how it is. I'm free out here. I don't like enclosed spaces. There's no one to tell me what I'm doin' right and what I'm doin' wrong. Thing is, I'm not like your kind. And your kind always tells me how I'm supposed to be. I've gotta do it my way or no way. You know why I play here?"

I shrugged.

"Look over there," he said pointing with his bow to a bronze statue. "Beethoven. He inspires me to play. Ludwig is the man." I'd never noticed the statue was Beethoven.

Everett's clear refusal to continue to be my raison d'être left me peering into the abyss of meaninglessness again.

"You gotta find your own way, Newspaper Man. Maybe it's time to figure out the essentials," Everett advised me one scorching October day as we stood next to Ludwig.

So, I did just that. I told my wife she was in charge of the reward money, and although she said with fists on her hips that spending it or investing it should be a team effort, she had no problem unilaterally allocating the funds in practical ways—college tuition fund, retirement fund, home improvement fund, and an emergency fund. Much better her than me. I would have taken a sabbatical, kissed my wife and girls goodbye, and ridden a Hog around the world. Hell, twice around, if my money held out. This demonstration on the micro-level reminded me that women are much better suited to responsible decision-making, and, once again, I wondered why it was mostly men running the world.

Instead of frittering away the reward money, I researched the Stradivarius tradition further and pitched a nonfiction book to my agent titled *Divine Strings*—exploring the divine in the arts through the Stradivarius lineage. With my publishing credits and high-profile agent, there was a bidding war and I landed an impressive book deal.

After the deal was signed, sealed, and delivered, I requested a meeting with the editor-in-chief at the *Times*.

"But who will do your column?" he inquired.

"I imagine no one after it hits the chopping block. I can't bear to watch the progressive amputation of this organism. Once the vital organs go, it's not long for the world. Who are we kidding? You know it, and I know it."

"Your column is still one of our most popular features."

"Don't they say it's better to leave the game when you're on top?"

"We need you, Ben."

"Not as much as you think."

And, after twenty-five years of writing a weekly column, that was that.

A couple of years after leaving the *Times*, I parked my car by Roosevelt Park to go listen to Everett and his four-stringed violin. En route to Beethoven's tunnel, I walked by a newspaper stand and froze in my tracks. The headline read: "L.A. Times to Replace Print with Web-based Format."

It had finally happened. The print version had gone the way of the dinosaur. What was next? Homo sapiens, perhaps?

I bought a copy as a historical keepsake, feeling the paper between my fingers, thinking about how much I'd now miss the bleeding newsprint on my smudged fingers. Would I ever adjust to screen glare and the lack of tactile sensation I felt while holding the flimsy newsprint in front of me and flipping the pages with a feeling of progress? When I made it to the classifieds, I always felt a smug sense of completion. How would I mark completion with scroll bars and clicks on endless links, photos, and headlines?

I had successfully jumped into a book publishing lifeboat, but Kindle, e-books, and related products were sharks that encircled my flimsy inflatable raft. For now, I could still create tangible works of art.

As I folded the paper—my paper—and stuck it underneath my arm, it struck me that Everett was not the only one who had been two strings short of a complete violin.

A Heart Never Broken

He shouldn't have been hoping what he was hoping. Although his mind was muddled, and his energy flagging, Simon knew in any other context what he wished for would have signified a deep, underlying disturbance. A circumstantial psychopath, he reclined in his multipurpose bed, one part entertainment center, another part cafeteria, library, and pharmacy, but mostly incarceration on a Posturepedic. Simon had grown to abhor pillows, discomforters, scratchy sheets, and the flat bouncy surface of his mattress. When he survived this ordeal, if he survived, he would eliminate beds from his life. How, he wasn't sure. Perhaps he'd live in a yurt and sleep on the cold, hard dirt.

It wasn't that his gray hairs had overtaken the auburn ones and that his sideburns and beard were so wizened that his grayish pallor was one layer of skin away from uncovering a Day of the Dead dancing skeleton. With his glasses on, he was a Dickensian scholar-ghost hybrid. So as to not daily spook himself, Simon draped sheets over every reflective surface in his house.

Simon spent untold hours peering at the medieval-style stained gold and ruby glass panel Sophia had handcrafted for him while studying mosaics in Florence. It featured hands reaching up, cradling a winged heart on the verge of releasing it. When the morning sun shone through, he was convinced the heart was just about to take flight. But when darkness fell, the heart was firmly ensconced in the hands; if they had let go, the heart would have plunged into an abyss of defective hearts. He was annoyed with Sophia for designing an image that planted doubt in his mind. But she had crafted it and they had installed it together when a winged heart had a completely different meaning. Simon considered obscuring it with a tapestry, but he couldn't bear to stamp out Sophia's presence completely.

As the weeks wore on, solitude had downgraded to solitary confinement. His bed, he had once joked, was a pleasure palace of carnal delights. "Now the only thing sharing my bed is a medical alert beeper," he would tell anyone willing to listen, which at this point was mostly medical types who were paid to care.

With each passing day and each emerging symptom— bone-deep fatigue, heart murmurs, dizziness, and swelling in his fingers and toes—his thoughts ventured where no man's mind should go. He envisioned all the mountain biking, kayaking, rock climbing, skateboarding, drag racing, and motorcycling going on outside as he laid in wait. Simon willed one such activity, just one, to go awry in the nick of time. He was a vulture of a man, circling his prey, waiting to swoop down to a strewn-out carcass on an empty expanse of highway.

In seconds, a nameless, faceless beating heart would be plucked out. And plunged into deep freeze.

Which is what he imagined could happen to his fragile heart if he continued to bestow it to his precious Sophia with waist-long gold-spun hair, intense green-blue eyes, and calloused artisan hands. His Sophia, the atheistic glass artist, commissioned by churches, temples, and cathedrals to create windows to the world for believers. He jested with her about crafting Jesus, Mary, and Moses glass when she viewed them as false prophets and posers—objects of worship that led people to rise up in rage-filled intolerance. Composition in beveled stained glass through which the sun's rays created fractals and lulled worshipers into a sense of goodwill toward men if only for the length of the service. Pouring out of the pews no longer peering through the mystical prism, believers' religious myopia returned.

That's what Sophia had said she adored about Simon; he was pure goodness. And a heart broken—not by love or life—but by pure bad luck.

In an act of self-preservation, after watching Sophia sleep for hours, Simon had walked out on her on a blustery night without an umbrella or slicker or Wellies and plodded for miles along a deserted beach littered with sea-carved driftwood and tangled strands of seaweed. He'd resisted returning to her arms, despite her imagined tearful pleas. Given what was at stake, Simon couldn't help but flash back on Sophia's first and, possibly not last, betrayal.

As a saucy tango dancer, Sophia had been courted by tangoistas wherever she danced. Once when she attended a tango intensive in Buenos Aires, she and her instructor tangoed off the dance floor and into his cabana, something from which Simon had still not recovered. He had wished Sophia would stop dancing while he was increasingly incapacitated, but he would never ask her to choose between him and tango. So, he made the choice for her.

Simon had to be preemptive, protective of his failing pump. Just how many beats were left in it, he didn't know. Any beat could be its last. He couldn't risk his heart with anyone, not even Sophia. His mantra became: better an ache than a break.

When his friend, Amelia and her version of the British invasion strode into his homebound medical unit a couple times a week armed with Kentucky Fried Chicken, cream-filled donuts and hours upon hours of British comedies tucked in her satchel, she brought Simon relief from the roulette wheel guessing game.

"The Colonel's greasy bits again?" He attributed her obsession with KFC to her lack of it as a girl growing up in the English countryside, and to its similarity to greasy, paper-wrapped fish and chips.

"Simon, you might as well live it up now. If this is it, why not enjoy it? If it's not, you'll have a new ticker to replace the one that you've subjected to grease and grime. It's a win-win."

Amelia was furiously texting while setting up their picnic on his bed. She belonged to the class of multitaskers that Simon frowned upon—never able to enjoy simple pleasures, one activity at a time. He feared he was a dying breed, soon to be an ancient artifact of a less frenzied era.

"Is my company not enough for you? Must you do that low-life activity in my presence? What are you saying that just can't wait? 'I'm eating KFC with a shut-in? Rescue me!'"

She glanced up from her phone. "Simon, stop! You need to get with the program. It's basically text or die." Then she

49

froze and said, "I didn't mean it like that…I just mean, hop on the train to the future."

"If that's the future, I'll stay on the platform, thank you."

Their friendship was still fresh at the time. They had known each other only a few months when Simon's condition had deteriorated to bedridden with a beeper. He had prepared for Amelia to jump ship, as had most of his friends, but amazingly, she endured without evenings on the town, adventurous escapades, and meanderings through the cityscape. Bed, bath, and no beyond.

Now even before she plunked down in the uneasy chair, as she called it, Amelia munched on an extra-crunchy chicken leg. "Do you think you'll have a change of heart?"

"That's the whole idea."

"No, about life and love and matters of the heart, you silly goose.

"I'll only change the slab of meat in my chest. So, no."

"I don't recognize that work. Which American poet are you quoting, Simon? It's got to be one of yours; we Brits would never be so vulgar."

"The beefniks, of course."

"Word to the wise: don't try to seduce anyone with that line."

"Noted."

"It may be a slab to you, but I cherish it."

"Do you want me to have them pickle it for you? I'm sure that could be arranged."

Simon's face stretched into a grin—a sensation that occurred so infrequently, he held the pose.

Amelia laughed. "Good thing I'm on to the donut course. I couldn't stomach this while eating breast meat." Amelia rolled her eyes while reaching into the donut box for one with colorful sprinkles. "I was reading about this middle-aged white chap who received a heart from a young African-American guy. The recipient was surprised by his newfound love of classical music. What he discovered was that the donor, who loved classical music and played the violin, had died in a drive-by shooting, holding his violin case to his chest. What if you start having random cravings or new talents, or even a new personality? Cool—huh?"

"That's a fairy tale, Amelia. A heart is a just a heart."

In the early morning hours on his fifty-seventh day of being bedridden, when the sun had yet to make its flashy debut and nearly launch his winged heart, Simon's sleep was interrupted by an insistent electronic beeping. In his dream that still lingered, he was hooked up to a heart monitor. "Don't let it flatline! Don't let it flatline!" he repeated frantically to Sophia, who was hovering at the foot of his bed modeling a sexy nurse's uniform circa 1950, not a live person, but a mannequin who couldn't save him.

When Simon realized he wasn't truly perishing in the company of Sophia, the figurine, he discovered the source of the interruption—his beeper flashing, vibrating, and beeping like a mini emergency unit. At long last, his sole constant companion, his promise of restored health, his lifeline was doing what it was meant to do, signaling the time had come. A part of him hoped it never would for the sake of the unlucky donor.

Don't ask for whom the beeper beeps; the beeper beeps for thee looped in his mind as paramedics whisked him into the ambulance and off to the cardiac transplant unit.

Once in pre-op, events unfolded like a film clip in fast forward. IV in, anesthesia mask on. Before Simon went under, he rehearsed in his head what would happen while he was out. Seven hours. Split open and splayed out on a table, the cardiac surgery team detaching the old and reattaching the new.

Four days later and finally strong enough to breathe on this own, Simon was transferred from the ICU to the transplant unit. The pain medication had worn off and a searing pain ripped down his sternum, leaving him breathless and motionless on an electric bed, which, if it had any more functionality, might actually fly.

In the transplant unit, nurses scurried, hovered, and positioned devices. They turned dials up and turned dials down, switched regulators on and switched them off, quibbled over their menu for a staff barbecue, and discussed money-saving home-improvement ideas. It took all Simon's reserve energy to utter, "More pain medication. Please." A raspy whisper, breaking the silence after four days of intubation.

A shadow crept over him, obscuring the green-white fluorescent light pouring down. Simon squinted his eyes to discover the cardiac surgeon towering over his bed, poised to deliver his ebullient post-op report.

"How are you feeling? You did good, Simon. You did really, really good, old boy. And you'll be happy to know I got you a good one."

"A good one?" Simon's voice was rough. He didn't have the energy to clear his throat.

"A good heart."

What was the proper response to that comment? "Oh." Surely, he could do better than that, given that the guy had saved his life. "Thank you, Doc. From the bottom of my new heart." Simon was relieved he could pull off a little levity.

Dr. Brock, the cardiac surgeon, a short man with a big man's presence, lowered his exuberant voice to a hush and leaned in. "Listen, Simon, I'm going off-record to tell you this, but I thought you'd be happy to know that you're now the proud owner of a fifteen-year-old heart."

A good ten seconds passed as Simon resisted this jarring newsflash with all his might. "Uh…A fifteen-year-old?" He wanted to share the doctor's enthusiasm for a fresh heart, but he couldn't prevent himself from reacting. Simon's eyes fluttered; he felt flushed and a little faint, and tried in vain to mask his horror. "Good God." A heart's a heart, he reminded himself to stave off the cascade of guilt and regret. It was the handiwork of twisted fate that a kid's unthinkable tragedy was his luck.

"Just like that, you're new and improved! You'll be up and running in no time."

"Doc, you've given me my life back." Although it wasn't the doctor's work securing the raw goods, just the painstaking insertion.

"Me and the snowboarder."

"Huh?"

In a hushed voice, the surgeon said, "Snowboarder upside down in a tree well. Poor boy. Probably didn't suffer long, though." Then, in a whispered exclamation, "And shazam! You're as good as new." The doctor gently socked him in the bicep.

Simon was certain the doctor would have insisted upon a high-five if he had been able to muster it.

"If you need anything, let Kate the Great know—okay?"

On cue, a nurse dressed in green scrubs with red hair pulled back, a baby face, and high color in her cheeks appeared over his bed. She didn't fit her moniker; instead she looked more like Kind Kate.

"How you doing, sweetie?" she asked as she prepared to shove a thermometer in his mouth.

"Honestly?"

"Sure. Try me. I've heard it all."

"Queasy." He tried to shift in the bed. "Dizzy."

"Open," she ordered with a grin and inserted the thermometer. "The doc said everything went perfectly, Simon. The dizziness and nausea is the anesthesia's after-effects. Sometimes it takes days for it to wear off."

He tried to talk through the slit in his mouth, but she shushed him. "We need an accurate reading. It will only take a minute." She paused and said, "Okay, open." She extracted the thermometer and read it. "Good. Very good."

"Couldn't they have found a better match?"

"They found a perfect match for you. It has to be perfect; otherwise, it won't take."

"No, I mean someone with more life under his belt. He was only fifteen. Just a kid. I should have given him my heart. Not the other way around."

"It's not a heart match dating service. As you can imagine, the heart harvesting process is completely random. Whatever comes in that day is what you get. Just think of it as the catch of the day!" Realizing she might have sounded a little glib, she added, "Don't worry yourself with it. That's how it works. Anyway, the doc shouldn't have told you about the donor. You're not supposed to know."

"He was snowboarding. Just out for a day of kicks. God knows how many of those days I've miraculously lived through. Thousands," said Simon.

Kate's gaze fell, and then she busied herself adjusting tubes and latches and the IV drip bag. "My boy is a boarder."

Simon grabbed her arm with his IV-injected hand, like a corpse coming to life. "Tell him he can't; tell him about this boy and about me. Promise me you'll do that. If there's anything to learn from this, it's that."

Kate thought for a moment and looked as though she might agree to his directive, but then said, "We can't stop them from living."

"We can stop them from dying." He held her gaze.

Kate snapped back into nurse mode, adjusting Simon's bed downward and arranging his table, liquids forward, pills back. "You need to get some rest. It's going to be a long road to recovery, and you'll need all your strength and then some. Word to the wise, don't worry yourself sick with this—okay?

You're not out of the woods yet. Do this boy a favor by seeing to it that his heart does the trick for you." With that, she flicked off the lights, whisked the curtain around his bed, and disappeared.

Simon drifted into a pain-medication-pumped slumber.

At 3:12 a.m., Simon awoke from a dream in which he was trapped in a burning house. When he came to, he realized that his chest was ablaze. All he could think about was dousing it with ice water to extinguish the flame. He was convinced that this is what heart rejection felt like. He buzzed the nurse on call, holding the button down until someone appeared.

A towering African-American woman appeared. "Yes?"

"I c-c-c-can't. I d-d-don't. Ohhhh."

"Okay, take it slowly. What's going on?

"I, my, it's burning. It's not right. S-s-something's wrong."

She scanned the room. "What do you mean?"

He pointed to his heart. "I think I'm rejecting…"

She nodded. "Ah. Pain's bad? Real bad? Right?"

Simon nodded.

"It's not a rejection. It's normal."

"You c-c-c-call this…? This pain is not normal! I'm dyyying here. In fact, I'd like to."

"That's crazy. We can get your pain down. Anything else?"

"I need Kate."

"She's gone home for the night. Is there something I can do for you?"

"It's just that, this kid. I didn't want to do this to a kid."

"I see where this conversation is headed. You didn't do anything to anybody. Give this pain pump time and you'll be good to go. Alrighty, then?"

The truth was his heart, the boy's heart, ached for the boy, for himself.

Kate gently tugged the curtain open, letting in the morning light. "Simon, you wanted to talk to me?"

"Yes. The nurse on the night shift didn't want any part of this. I must get it off my chest.

"Shoot."

"I don't feel like myself."

"Of course, you don't. You just had a heart transplant."

"No, not physically. Mentally. I'm thinking too much about this heart."

"That's normal."

"I don't think this is going to work."

"What do you mean?"

"What if it has never been broken?"

"What if what hasn't been broken?"

"The heart."

Kate sighed and said, "It's yours now. Like you bought a used car. The owner signs over the ownership. And you can do with it whatever you wish."

"But don't you see? I have what very few people have—a heart that has never been broken with the wisdom gained from a broken heart many times over. How would I do it differently if given a clean slate?"

"My guess is you wouldn't do it any differently the second, third, or fourth time around."

"I'm the keeper of his heart. I must be careful with a heart so tender, a heart so young. I can't be reckless with it."

"How are you going to manage that in the messy business of love?" asked Kate. And then she added, "Don't forget that you've arrived in this place because he was reckless with his body. I know that may sound insensitive, but it's true." Kate began her morning routine of checking all his vitals—blood pressure, temperature, and heart rate.

Simon asked, "What if I reject this heart?"

Kate shrugged her shoulders. "It happens. Then you'll have to get another one. Let's hope you'll be as lucky the second time around. But to ensure that this heart has a fighting chance, we'll make sure your daily immune-suppression regime goes without a hitch."

"Not my body—me."

Kate's eyes locked onto Simon's and she leaned against his bed. "You're kidding—right? You think you could reject this heart, even if your body doesn't?" Her whole body slumped as if diminishing patience were draining her life force. "If you'll allow me to say this, I think you have too much time to think. You need to do something to occupy yourself—books, movies, computer games. Seriously, this could drive you nuts. It's a done deal, Simon." And before leaving, she added with insistence, "None of this is going to bring him back. You know that—right? It's up to you to live your life now that you've been given a second chance. If I were you, I'd do something with it."

When she left the room, he stared straight ahead. She was right; he should busy himself to take his mind off matters of his heart. He had brought Pulitzer-Prize-winning *Guns, Germs, and Steel* to polish off during his recovery. As he reached for the book, the screen of his iPhone on the bedside table beckoned him to distraction.

He picked it up and was inexplicably drawn to the games and apps icon. When he touched it, hundreds of game selections displayed. His eyes locked on Rhino Ball, Critter Crunch Lite, and Space Buster—all absurd-sounding applications he and Sophia would have ridiculed, pointing out that it was further evidence of the downfall of modern society—the electronic equivalent of Roman frivolity and excess.

What if? A bolt of panic shot through his body.

After playing several rounds of Critter Crunch Lite and Rhino Ball and rocketing through countless game levels, Simon navigated to text messages, uncharacteristically tempted by the ease of communication. He clicked Create New Message, scrolled down his contact list as if suddenly an expert, and slowed as he approached P, Q, R, S. Sasha, Sara, Selma, Solidad, Sophia.

Upon seeing her name, Simon's new heart skipped, fluttered, and then beat wildly in his beleaguered chest. His torso stiffened—bracing, protecting his pump, waiting for it to seize up and falter. But it pumped with vigor; it pumped with might.

Inching further into the forbidden realm, Simon composed. Her eyes, his words, her heart.

As he crafted the message, the boy's heart safely nestled beneath his rib cage, soared, plunged, skated up and around a loop-de-loop, and landed, navigating the terrain with intimate grace.

Cookies of Fortune

Trudging on the abandoned pedestrian walkway, I scanned the illuminated Golden Gate Bridge in its burnt sienna architectural glory arching toward the wooded Presidio. No doubt the bridge architects and engineers had envisioned a functional beauty spanning, connecting, and teeming with transitions, not a whistling siren of death for lost souls.

I toted fortune cookies in my backpack and braced against a maritime gust carrying a pungent mix of saline, eucalyptus, and car exhaust. It whipped the hair islands by my ears and chilled the crown of my head. The elements were unkind to balding men like me. My bushy mustache warmed my upper lip, which didn't require warming. I had hair everywhere but where I wanted it, where it would have benefited me in becoming a ladies' man or even a man's man.

But I didn't mind. I was in the business of making people laugh.

I could usually detect the ones I had come for from across the bridge. Their silhouettes, alone and lingering, as if undecided, as if wrestling with their life force, as if snuffing it out was against their nature. The agitated ones paced like captive cougars. The subdued were statuesque in a standing meditation. All studied the rolling waves as if waiting for a message to emerge from the sea. As if waiting for just the right swell, just the right gust, just the right lull. Or perhaps they didn't even see the water. Scenes from their lives leading up to this moment played like a slideshow captured with a shadowy lens, images overlaying the ghostly sea below. Hardly ever did they take in the panoramic view, the expanse of the bridge, or the sparkling islands of civilization at each end.

They never looked up.

That's how I knew. Tourists peered away from the water, because it held nothing for them at nightfall. Except phantoms. And tourists didn't come for phantoms. They came for the bright lights, big city, the wow, the world of awe, of wonder, of thrill and excitement.

The older jumpers fancied themselves wise about love and life. But collecting life experiences had a way of making them foolish. They said this: sometimes the pain wouldn't cease, sometimes life let them down in unimaginable ways, sometimes there was no escape from evil, often ennui had settled in for good. I thought them unwise for permanently trading in hope for despair.

They could take all night, which was okay. I had all night to give.

The older ones didn't want to try again. Trying is what had turned their lives into shambles in the first place. I pressed them to divulge until they were so weary their empty beds beckoned more than the sea. If I could get them to morning, I'd have won.

The young ones were the easiest. They'd experienced a single heartbreak, bullying, or parents gone awry, and, because they were untainted, the virgin pain seared. What they didn't know yet was the pain would cease. It was my job to teach them. It took no time to persuade the young ones that all endings weren't bad. And that all bad endings fade. If we just let them. Hope was just a whisper away.

On this night, a gaunt young man in a dark hoodie and sagging pants leaned over the bridge railing with a piece of paper trembling in his hands. I approached him from behind.

"May I read it?" I asked.

"Who the fuck are you?" He wadded his paper and stuffed it in his hoodie pocket.

"Someone who wants to know why before, not after."

"Fuck no. Get lost, dude."

"I'm not going anywhere until you tell me why."

He groaned.

With young guys, it was almost always about a girl. "What's her name?"

"Jasmyn. Spelled with a y-n. That's how she always said it anyway."

"And you are?"

"Jason spelled like it sounds. Uncomplicated."

"Did she break your heart?"

"You could say that."

"Left you for another guy?"

"She jumped from here a year ago, okay? Happy now?"

It socked me in the gut, but dwelling on it could make me lose another. "So your plan is to join her? Have you ever thought that she might want you to live the life she can't?"

"No, not really."

"What made her so special?"

"Oh, I don't know."

"Please. Try."

He glanced down at his heart. "I don't know why I'm telling this to some random dude. Her Woody the Woodpecker laugh. The way she slurped her sesame noodles. The way she flipped her hair when she was nervous. The way

66

she composed hilarious poems from fortune cookies. I can't even look at a fortune cookie."

I just happened to have one on me. I reached into my pack and offered him an individually wrapped cookie.

"Why are you doing this?" he asked.

"Please, just open it, and eat it, if you'd like."

He snatched it, tore it open, and crushed it, shoving the pieces into his mouth as if he hadn't eaten for days.

"Now read the fortune," I said.

"Seriously?"

"Please."

"It says, 'I think you just ate your fortune.'" The downturned corners of his mouth perked up and he snorted a chuckle. His eyes no longer squinted against pain. "She would have said something like: your fortune will pass and will soon come out of your ass." He shoved the fortune in his pocket. "I'm saving this one."

I knew I had him then.

Years later, I went searching for the man who had saved my life on the anniversary of Jasmyn's jump. I crisscrossed the bridge, scanning the glowing expanse for a character with dark hair protruding from both sides of his shiny head and a mustache that consumed his face. I wanted to thank him. For pulling me back from the edge, for getting me to believe in someone just long enough to start again, for helping me to remember, for giving me a fortune to hold onto, for getting me to see that joy can come again.

I returned to the bridge often but never spotted him. I started to wonder if he actually existed at all, or if I had created him to save my life. But I had the fortune he had given me. I wasn't just dreaming.

One blustery night when the creeping fog had settled around my coatless body like a blanket of frost, I spotted an old guy with a pea coat and a newsboy cap who mirrored me on my jump night—on the edge, slumped yet determined. I ran to him and asked him if he needed someone to talk to. He said not a word but shook his head and extended his hand in a stay-away gesture.

Ever since my experience, I carried fortune cookies in my knapsack. I offered him one. He refused by shaking his head. I insisted, forcing the cookie into his hand, curling my fingers around his, and asked him to read it aloud.

At first, he didn't resist my touch but then snatched his hand back, keeping the cookie.

"Don't be ridiculous," he grumbled. "What am I going to do with a fortune?" He pointed to himself and then gestured toward the water, ending his demonstration with a you-complete-moron expression.

He didn't intimidate me. "Oh, go on. Just give it a try."

He held out his hand with the cookie to try to give it back.

I shoved my hands into my pockets so he could see they were out of commission. Then I held his gaze to let him know I understood his pain.

His hands trembled as he struggled to remove the wrapper. He finally broke into it with his teeth. A gust of wind sent the wrapper soaring toward the sea. His reflexes were far too sluggish to catch the airborne plastic.

"Darn it. I hate littering." He cracked the cookie, and extracted the fortune. Then he glanced up at me, with child-like eyes looking for encouragement.

"Read it to me. Please."

"Okay. Here goes. Help! I'm a prisoner in a Chinese bakery!" He read, his voice raspy. For a moment, he forgot where he was and let out a hearty belly laugh.

I knew I had him then.

I told him my own story as we walked away from the sea in the squalling wind. He offered me his coat and said he didn't mind feeling chilly if it meant he was still alive.

I watched that night as Jason escorted a would-be jumper to safety. It reminded me of a dark December morning years ago when my head of hair was full but my heart empty. I had one running shoe on the bridge's railing and the other on the ground, poised to spring up and over. Someone yanked my leg just as my shoe was about to bounce up from the surface of the bridge.

I caught my balance and spun around to see a pudgy man offering me a fortune cookie. "Please. Open it."

So furiously amused by this interloper's prank, I didn't even think to resist his absurd request. When I cracked the cookie in two and pulled out the thin strip of paper, I squinted to read the tiny words as I munched the cookie's sweet crunchy goodness. My fortune said: the fortune you seek is in another cookie.

He had me then. I needed to find that other cookie.

The Era of Lanterns and Bells

No one ever stays.

And so, I've grown to despise the sea. The sea is a siren of death, and the air an alchemist of spirits. Together, they give birth to maritime phantoms. I'm no longer a lighthouse that directs ships, but a tower that attracts lost souls. During gale-force winds and tumultuous storms, my lantern tower casts an amber glow and my whistle blows, even though my parts stopped functioning years ago.

I'm quite a remarkable structure, actually. I'm the highest point on Raspberry Island, and I look as though I belong in a Gothic romance. I'm an offshore wave-swept tower atop a reef of sunken rocks and subjected to the wrath of the sea. My fifty-two-foot tower looks like a giant candy cane—swirling red and white peppermint stripes—now fading, licked by the sea. My light is a first-order Fresnel lens with

1,009 prisms and was installed in 1880. My lens could throw light twenty miles to the horizon.

The trouble began with Violet during the era of lanterns and bells. Violet was the wife of Edgar, a lighthouse keeper who lived here in the 1880s. When Violet first arrived, she was mesmerized by the breaking waves below and the shifting cloud patterns above. Then, by the third full moon, she started to climb up and down my stairs, pace in my lantern room, wring her hands, and rock herself to sleep. She was tired of the sea and clouds and edgy from the wind. After her restless period came the raging period. She slammed my doors, locked herself in my tower, and threatened to plunge into the sea from my deck. Violet screamed, "Tower of torture," over and over again. Naturally, I didn't take to her. Then, like a dense fog that never lifts, melancholy set in. This is when Edgar sent for a piano.

It seemed that the baby grand was the answer for both Violet and Edgar. Violet would no longer pressure Edgar to leave—to return to the town where she was so happily surrounded by fellow musicians and artists. But Violet only had one piece of sheet music, which she played repeatedly— sometimes from the red sky at night until the twinkle of dawn. The couple quarreled about the music, but Violet said she was playing the sea; her music reflected the monotony of the waves. At last she could convey to Edgar how the salted sea had pickled her mind. The pickling must have spread to Edgar's as well. On a night of freezing fog when feathery ice crystals coated the decks and railings, Edgar threw an axe over his shoulder and climbed the tower to the piano room. He chopped the mahogany piano to bits. Then he crept down to the bedroom and took an axe to Violet. I was all for it, until he turned the axe on himself. Unfortunately, no one shredded the music. Like a piece of driftwood that forever bobs in the water, the melody surges and recedes with the tides. Some say you can hear it when listening to shells that wash up on shore.

In the era of lanterns and bells, I was a sight to behold— fresh red and white paint, polished brass and ironwork, a sparkling lens, and a bell that pierced thick blankets of fog. I guided countless ships and crafts to shore and comforted thousands of wayfaring captains. I had a valiant purpose—to see to it that lives, commerce, and crafts were preserved.

Now I'm just a house of gulls. I'm streaked and spotted with gull droppings that glue fish bones, scales, and feathers to my decks, sills, and roof. The gulls torment me with their squawking and circling. If only I could be a scarecrow.

After Edgar and Violet, there was a succession of keepers who were driven away by Violet's monotonous melody. One keeper didn't mind the ethereal music so much as the repetition of the same piece. If there had been a varied

73

ghostly repertoire, he might have stayed on. Two nights before his departure, he cried out to the phantom pianist in his sleep, requesting Chopin's Nocturne. The ghost of Violet didn't oblige.

I was deserted once again.

Then came Carlotta and Sven Jensen, a Scandinavian couple, during the era of the new Fresnel lens. Sven drowned just days after taking the job when his dinghy capsized in whitecaps. The celebratory glogg he and Carlotta had been drinking had gone to his head. "Don't go out when the wind is blowing 50 knots," I wanted to say. Carlotta returned to Stockholm a widow. She blamed me for taking her husband. But it was the sea. The wretched sea.

Mac arrived in 1923 after Sven Jensen's death. I thought he might be a keeper. I sensed it was love at first sight. He would spend his days scrubbing my decks, polishing my windows and brass, and replacing broken parts. Mac would balance precariously on ladders, adding a fresh coat of brick-red paint to my exterior walls and ivory to my window frames. He kept the lens and windows so clean that the light would not be weakened. Polishing the lens could take eight hours a day, but this wasn't a problem for Mac, who never slept. I sparkled under his keep. My light beamed at its full intensity at night, and my foghorn pierced thick, floating fog—providing direction to wayward ships and crafts.

Ten years to the day he first arrived, Mac learned that his wife had run off with a one-eyed captain of an island ferry, a pirate, people said. Mac stood perched on my upper deck contemplating his final jump. "No, don't do it! We'll find another lighthouse missus," I wanted to say, but lighthouses can't talk. I couldn't stop him. He fell to his death from my upper deck to which he had just applied a new veneer. I hoped the sea would cradle and return him to me, but the sea was his tomb. The damned sea.

Mac's ghost sometimes scrubs my decks, turns my foghorn off and on, and fixes broken lights. And several captains have been mysteriously guided to shore when their vessels were lost at sea.

Mac is a benevolent ghost.

I am now a wandering eye with no mooring, a Cyclops of the sea. The howling wind seeps through the cracks in my walls, doors, and window frames. When the wind blows more than one-hundred knots, a high-pitched squeal echoes through my structure. During storms, my creaks are so intense it feels as if I'm going to crack in half, but I never do. When the driving rain assaults my tower, water forms pools and rivulets on my worn and buckling hardwood floors. There's no one to place buckets under the leaks to catch the water. I'm rotting from the inside out.

People don't know what to do with me anymore. If I had my say, I'd be a freshly painted candy-cane lighthouse throwing light across the water, lit up by a watchful keeper and his wife. But now lighthouses are automated and monitored electronically by the U.S. Coast Guard. Some say that the trend to automate and abandon lighthouses is because personnel won't serve in haunted lighthouses. Now it's just me and a bevy of ghosts.

The local chamber of commerce is considering placing me on a tour of haunted lighthouses. There's talk of a gift shop with nautical knick-knacks. Goose-bump-seeking tourists with floppy hats, lighthouse ghost-buster T-shirts, dangling digital cameras, and bright white tennies will climb my tower, expecting ghosts to open doors, creak floors, perform beheaded hovering, and moan in eerie tones. But tourists don't understand ghosts the way I do. Ghosts don't perform on cue. They only show you signs when you least expect it—to make believers of nonbelievers.

Lucky me. After one hundred years of lighting the sea for sailors, I've become a haunted house. That is why I hate the sea. It made ghosts of men who cared for me.

Hole in the Wall

The beeping forklift backed up to Celeste's two-story French Tudor house where a hole would soon be carved out of the storybook facade by the demolition team. She had instructed them to make the hole neat and tidy, but after hearing her body dimensions, the foreman had said, "We can do neat and tidy, but we can't do small."

"That's a given," she had said, a snort of derision masking her shame.

Celeste glimpsed quaking leaves and shifting clouds from her vantage point. She marked time from her sagging mattress by gazing at the framed portrait of life—bare branches and steely sky, verdant buds reaching for radiance, giant raindrops frolicking on foliage, raking light and golden leaves, and, if she was lucky, a crescent moon.

She detected rumbling motors and workmen's harried voices as the demolition and forklift crews situated themselves. She pictured the industrial equipment the way she imagined everything in a world unfolding without her. The sexing, birthing, toiling, thieving, lusting, frolicking world outside.

Freedom, she thought. At last.

As the workmen punched through her wall, panic seized her breath. The wall—as imprisoning as it was—had shielded her from the torching glare of humanity and its hasty assumptions. Remnants of the world outside had come to her—Diet Cokes, casseroles, pastries, medicine, thrillers, romances, and musicals. That had been a comfortable existence. Now strangers were about to emerge through the hole with the question etched on their faces. Celeste loathed the question. But if she didn't address it, people would fill in the blanks and cast scornful glances upon her.

Scorn was the one thing she couldn't bear.

Celeste wanted to say, "It could happen to you, too." She knew that was what people, especially women, feared. "It starts with just one box of glazed donuts, and then a multiplier effect takes hold."

Her anxiety wasn't so much anticipating the impending stares from the demolition crew; it was serving up a reason that would wipe their expressions clean. She thought she at least owed them a rationale. Or did she?

As they drilled, pounded, and penetrated, the breeze supplanted the stale air of her bedroom, a cacophony of odors: fermenting socks and musty underarms, vanilla and cinnamon clove potpourri, pot and patchouli, cigarettes and beer, coffee and chocolate.

She breathed in freshness.

Through the thick crumbling plaster, greenery and blooms emerged, the exuberant lilac tree's bursts of fragrance and the neighbor's cherry, lemon, grape lollipop garden—imported tulips—that she had bragged about during her weekly delivery of tuna noodle casseroles. Eight cheesy-fishy pies per week. Enough to feed a football team.

If it hadn't been for the casserole delivery, there wouldn't now be a gaping hole in the side of her house. During one of the drop-offs, her neighbor brought her six-year-old granddaughter, who stared unabashedly, but without the question heavy on her tongue. It was an altogether different one.

"Will you fly my dragon kite with me? Don't worry. It's not the scary kind. It's pretty pink and purple."

Her grandmother apologized with a comment, "Kids will be kids," and flailing hand gestures, whisking the girl out of the room to preempt other inappropriate remarks.

Celeste hadn't realized the extent to which she had been imprisoned by the question until another one was posed, a question not tinged with contempt, a question boundless, a question with wings. She pictured herself as the dragon, aloft with the breeze, climbing to dizzying heights. She soared, kissing the clouds, hugging the edge of treetops. As the currents beckoned her, she would glide and swirl, dive and twirl. When a strong draft tugged the dragon from the girl's hands, she was released.

Once Celeste had tasted the sweetness of flight, she made the call.

Inspecting parts of the yard she hadn't seen in years, she spotted her white lattice fence with climbing nasturtium wildly out of control, evidence that the gardener was collecting his weekly remittance while neglecting his duties. He assumed she would never know the difference from where she lay.

A bright yellow forklift carriage with a helmeted rider jerked through the hole like a dynamic component on a theatrical set. Perfectly timed, the reinforcement team exploded through her bedroom door. A crew of eight men with hazmat suits and preparedness stances surrounded her.

As though she were a bomb ready to detonate.

A string of explanations suited to her audience raced through her mind and teetered on the tip of her tongue. She sensed the shape of each one dancing in her mouth, none ready for prime time.

"Ready, set, deploy!" shouted the crew commander.

The crew slid and then yanked the tarp under her body, their gasps and grunts assaulted her, each one an unarticulated insult torpedoing through her core.

She realized this was the first time she had been touched in years. Had it not been so rough, it would have made her weep.

The tarp maneuvering process gave her more time to craft an answer to the question. The glandular rationale went over well. The public had heard such roving microphone confessions on Oprah and Jerry Springer. There was always the childhood trauma angle that elicited a cascade of pity and sympathy. Genetics were another viable route, but wrinkles of doubt formed and lingered in response.

Her preferred approach was one that resolved the line of questioning. But the thing everyone was thinking—that was what they wanted to hear.

The forklift driver positioned the forks underneath the tarp as the eight men heave-hoed. This was her last chance to answer the question. She could either breathe compassion into their steely work crew demeanors or feed their gluttonous curiosity.

Celeste inhaled sharply and half-whispered, "There's a hole that I can't patch alone."

"Yes, we're aware of that, ma'am," said the forklift rider. Then into his headset, he announced, "Casualty secured. Lower."

Touched by Fire

If only I hadn't left the pink flamingo raft behind. But sometimes life is like that. Seemingly mundane occurrences—losing your keys, forgetting your sunglasses, leaving your floatation device—can twist your fate until you don't recognize yourself. If only Jamaican beach vendors had peddled inflatables instead of weed. I would've been miles away, afloat in a permanent exhale, wispy sapphire arcing into shimmering turquoise.

It was a near collision in the glass-and-chrome hotel lobby, a tie-dyed bikini cover-up and I Love NY. But his T-shirt wasn't the first thing I noticed. I recognized him, a towering wild-haired swashbuckler. Not like I had actually seen him before.

"Do you?" I asked.

"Do I what?"

"Love New York?"

"Hell, no."

"Then why wear it?"

"They don't sell I Hate NY."

"They should."

"Who are you?" He already knew the answer and that scared me.

"I hate NY too."

"Can you feel this?" he grabbed me by the shoulders. Not a hostile grab. I think to test if I was real or make-believe.

"Yes. How could I not?"

"Holy crap. Come with me." He veered across the manicured lawn as if he knew I would follow.

"Where are you going?" I caught myself. "Wherever it is, I can't."

"I'm getting on a bus now. You have to come."

"Can't you take the next one?"

He grasped my hand and pulled me under a flowering ginger lily tree. We sat cross-legged, knees touching, Namaste. He was salt, coconut, jasmine, and I cherry, basil, and pepper.

"I had to leave New York, which is why I'm here."

"You live here?"

"Come. Be with me."

A tingle swept from his legs to mine, my pulse ignited my mind. *Could I?*

84

He reached for me. I pushed his hand to my heart, aching for the softness of his fingertips and the sharpness of his nails. He strummed me like an ancient, delicate instrument not quite nearing dust.

Play me. I've heard your song for years.

"I must go."

I tickled his palm with my number.

"Sing it to me instead."

I whisked his cheek with my mermaid hair—corkscrews, seaweed, and salt. He exhaled wild sage and coriander.

"I just met him." I was breathless from moving the sea beneath my inflatable flamingo.

"Who?" said my girlfriend, floating on a blown-up sea shell, conch pink suspended on translucent aquamarine. Our rafts kissed then parted.

"My soulmate."

She plunged her hand into the Caribbean Sea and splashed me. Droplets cooled my skin. "Don't hoard all the good stuff." But that wasn't it.

I rolled into the water, pulled the raft under my breasts, and flutter-kicked back to her. "He's been with me for a long time."

"I know. I feel it too. Jamaica will do that do you. What's his name?"

I knew him so well, I had forgotten to ask. "Jamaica."

Jamaica was inside me. Pine cones weren't seashells, conifers not palm trees. I would dream the sea and wake up to the mountains. Willing my phone to ring made it fall silent. I buried it under the couch to forget. But I could sense its burn through the cushions.

He came to me mostly in song. Sometimes in rain. Often in a flash of color. Then in a ring tone.

"I was afraid I had lost you."

"Come. Be with me."

"It's not that easy. I have a life."

"Don't let your life stop you from being you."

I tried to forget. Ivy snaked through my dreams and threatened to choke me in thatched vines and leaves. I dialed Jamaica.

"Is this the lady with the life?"

"It's the song. I can't stop the song."

"Yes, I know. Come. Be with me."

And I did. Leave the world of bills, appointments, and deadlines. Vinyasa retreat by the sea, I professed. To find my way back, even though I hadn't realized I was lost.

And I did. Find my way back. The sand shifted, cradled, glazed our bodies, writhing, reaching, settling. Salt water buoyed our rhythms, a circular motion, surging and receding, pushing and pulling to ecstatic depths. The sea cried me. He craved salt.

The wind howled and swirled the ocean. My toes clawed the sand, my hair whipped and blinded me; a storm propelled my cries over furious whitecaps.

I left him without a word, without a trace. Words would bind me to the life he knew I wanted. Each time, a part of me was cleaved and buried in Jamaica.

I had learned his name: Ethan Anderson.

I slumbered without dreams. No one knew the difference. He came to me in distress. I awoke and dialed.

"Cooh deh, dem ah galang lakka seh dem nuh ha nutten." Right country. Wrong man.

I hung up and redialed. "Jamaica. Is it you?"

"Mi am na well. Mi had to sell de drugs for de money. Breddah dem kill for drugs." *Had someone confiscated his phone?*

"Who is this?" I accused the interloper.

"Cum an be wid mi."

The surface underfoot, hardwood and marble, buckled. Walls with perched light sconces and framed paintings crumbled in slow motion. *I don't know you.* "I'm sorry." I hurled the Rastafarian stranger against the wall, his voice silenced by shattering electronic components.

The last time he came to me, it was in a newsflash.

American in Jamaica seized at the American Embassy. Went on a rampage, hurling backpack over the counter. Five days before President Obama due to arrive in Kingston. Security on high alert. Terrorist team called in. Terrorist threat checked out. Suspect hospitalized in what appeared to be a manic episode. Man identified as Ethan Anderson, an American living in Jamaica.

I felt the sea recede, not the tug of the tide by the phasing moon, but a fierce wrenching, a wild fire engulfing the waves, flames singeing the sky, a fountain of sparks raining ashes. The world faded to grey.

Standing beneath the shower, I noticed the streaming ashes were curiously shaped. Quarter notes, half notes, eighth notes followed by rests. Nothing but rests.

Swimming in Colors

As a girl growing up in Ashland, Massachusetts, I loved
to skinny dip in a purple pond. Well, the pond wasn't
always purple. It was also yellow, orange, red, green, and blue.
My friend Darcy liked when it was red. We'd compromise
and swim together when it was blue. On blue days, I
imagined a blue lagoon with cascading waterfalls and secret
coves for kissing. Darcy played the boy and I the girl.

One sun-drenched day, Darcy proudly displayed her
budding breasts and proclaimed, "Girls with breasts can't play
boys. You play the boy." I never saw myself as a boy, so I
refused. She spoiled the secret of the blue lagoon.

I regret not swimming on her red days. It's the least I
could have done for my sweet Darcy—to have dipped my
body in her favorite color. Now she's gone. She died of soft
tissue sarcoma the day before her twenty-sixth birthday. The
red pond had always reminded me of swimming in blood, as

though a living creature had been slaughtered, its blood staining the water. The pond rippled and lapped with red grief. She said that red was the color of passion—like hot cinnamon candies that tickled your tongue and roses with ribbons that boys brought when they said, "I love you."

I went alone on purple days. I'd sit among the tall grass and watch the purple stream pour into the pond like a river of grape juice. The plum-colored water lapped the banks, engulfing the reeds and lily pads. I'd imagine that a painter had just rinsed his paintbrushes after covering his canvas with lilacs or irises. My body became a living purple canvas. I'd plunge in and pretend I was a purple mermaid looking for a patched pirate with a treasure chest of jewels.

That was twenty years ago.

Last Thanksgiving, I was told by an impassive doctor in a white-washed room that I had a rare form of soft tissue sarcoma. The color drained out of my cheeks. "Cancer," I confirmed. I recognized the name—it was Darcy's cancer. *What were the chances of that?*

The doctor explained that my case was puzzling; no cancer in my family and no lifestyle choices would have caused my condition. "Sometimes cancer just happens," he explained. "Environmental toxins, mutations, or fate."

Fate, how scientific, I thought. "How long do I have?" I asked.

"Hard to say," he said. "Could be six months. Could be five years."

He explained that my options were to do nothing, start chemo immediately, or try an alternative light therapy. I imagined a lavender light healing me like the cleansing waters of my purple pond.

"I'll need to think about it."

After the news, I drove out to the pond to clear my mind. I hadn't been there since before Darcy's death. As I approached the bluff overlooking the pond, I noticed a neon-orange sign posted by the makeshift diving board and another by the tattered rope swing. I parked and walked over to the rope-swing sign, remembering all the times I straddled the scratchy rope, and released my body into the chilly blue and purple waters. It read: *Contaminated water. Do not swim, bathe or wade. Contact with the water may be life-threatening. Ashland Textiles, Inc.*

Red-hot anger welled up from my core. I wanted to run away from the now tainted memories and never return. But instead I strode over to the trunk of my car, which contained gardening tools. I opened the trunk, grabbed the shears and slammed the trunk, causing the car to shake. I marched back to the pond with my shears, like a soldier with a rifle in tow advancing to the frontline. When I reached the rope-swing tree, I dropped the shears on the ground. I grabbed the rope swing and pulled it as far from the pond as it would go. I jumped up and straddled the knot, feeling the familiar scratchy sensation on my inner thighs. I swung over the pond and back behind the tree, over the pond and behind the tree, until the swing came to a stop. Then I jumped off and wound the rope swing as tight as it could go. I positioned the knot between my legs, and leaned back as it spun me and the branches and sky above until dizziness set in. When the spinning stopped, I realized it was time. I couldn't delay any longer.

I picked up the shears and stared at the knot and the frayed rope underneath. I opened the shears and cut above the knot we had straddled so many times. I watched the knot fall to the ground. Then in a cutting frenzy, I cut the rope higher and higher until I couldn't reach anymore. Half a dozen segments of the frayed rope had fallen to the ground around me. It looked like a rope-swing massacre.

As I walked away, I thought that as the colors had washed over our bodies, painting our imaginations, they had bled our life force and left us colorless.

Fickle Grapes

According to some, he was one of those Oreo guys— black on the outside, white on the inside. He was resilient, witty as hell, and played people well. Poverty had made him strong. She was a Jewish mainliner, neurotic, unmedicated (unlike most other Jewish mainliners), with chaotic hair and a Jewish butt. Privilege had made her soft.

Her Jewish relatives made sure she never forgot those who perished in the concentration camps. They could be kibitzing at a deli, and Auschwitz would make its way in between the bagels and lox. She learned to carry her guilt in her tote bag. She could strike a guilty expression in two seconds flat. No one ever suspected faux guilt.

Rachel hadn't yet told her parents that Thomas was black. They knew he wasn't Jewish, which was bad enough. She had been programmed from conception that the only suitable boys were the Stewart Cohens, Bruce Bermans, and

Adam Steinbergs of the world. Of course, she was never the least bit interested in the boys in her Hebrew class. She had always been drawn to boys and men of color. First, it was Ricky Alvarado, a Hispanic. Then it was Ethan Lee, a Chinese-American. Now, it was Thomas James, a man with two first names from North Philadelphia—a neighborhood like Harlem before its renaissance.

When her parents saw her fondness for boys of color, they pulled her out of her diversity-tolerant Friends' school and put her in a Jewish school for girls. This gorging on all things Jewish made Rachel feel that if she added one more Jewish element to her life, she would die of Judaic gluttony.

The truth, according to her grandmother, was that any boy who wasn't Jewish was the enemy and would eventually side with the next Hitler of the world—because there was going to be one. Many Jews believed in the return of Hitler the way Christians believed in the rebirth of Christ. To Rachel, the lines between Hitler and the way Christians saw Jesus were blurred. Rachel tried to remind her grandmother that Hitler was Aryan, not black or Hispanic. This didn't seem to help. Every non-Jewish boy was a Hitler candidate. And any time Rachel dated a Hitler candidate, her grandmother sat anticipatory shivah, as though she was expecting Rachel's imminent death.

Rachel had intended to tell her parents many times about Thomas—after her cousin's bar mitzvah, after Seder dinner, at their family gathering at the Jersey shore, but there was never a good time. Her parents first approached the problem of the non-Jewish boyfriend by making innocuous suggestions.

"You know, Danny Aaron is single again. I can set you up. Just say the word," her mother would say. When that didn't work, they tried guilt. "Your uncle Abraham, God rest his soul, would have wanted to see you with a nice Jewish boy."

Why "nice" and "Jewish boy" were always coupled, Rachel didn't understand.

When all else failed, her parents tried scare tactics.

"Rebecca Horowitz married a cockamamy Wasp, who abducted the children during their divorce. They were found abandoned in the woods behind a trailer park in Alabama. A Jew would never do that. For God's sake, a sane Jew would never set foot in Alabama."

Rachel had had many conversations with herself—first motivational, then shaming, about breaking the news before the face-to-face meeting. She had let time slip through her fingers as she devised and rehearsed various angles. An angle would seem perfect, but would fall flat during the rehearsal.

"Remember the song, 'Ebony and Ivory'? That's like me and Thomas." Nope, too cheesy, like the song, she thought.

Then Rachel imagined pairing race with comments about the Rendell administration. "Thomas was the first African American appointed to the Rendell administration." Or perhaps this: "Thomas was the first black student from North Philly High to get a full scholarship to the Woodrow Wilson School of Public Policy at Princeton." Good angle. She'd slip it in among the accolades. She had managed to tell her parents all Thomas's accomplishments, but had sidestepped the racial bomb dropping.

As Thomas and Rachel approached her parents' door, she felt the sudden need for a panic attack dog. Where was her dog when she needed it?

If Rachel had let herself think rationally about the situation, she would have realized Thomas was exactly the kind of man her parents had hoped she would find—accomplished, witty, cultured, and compassionate. But she was certain her parents would object to the packaging. They always had a way of making her feel like she was doing the wrong thing. They never saw who she truly was. Around her parents, Rachel felt invisible.

Her father threw the door open.

"Dad, this is Thomas." Rachel's heart was developing a new arrhythmic pattern at her parents' doorstep.

"It's very nice to meet you, Thomas," her dad said without a hitch.

"You as well. To finally meet you after all the great things I've heard is my pleasure." Thomas was calm, using his most polished public policy persona.

"I'm sure the reviews have been mixed, knowing Rachel." Her father winked.

"Hannah, they're here," her father yelled down the hallway. Her mother scurried toward the door with a potholder in hand. She greeted Rachel with a peck on both cheeks and then said, "Where's Thomas?" looking for another person beyond the landing.

"This is Thomas."

Her mother stared at Thomas, as though she could will him to change into the person she had imagined. She clumsily shifted her potholder from one hand to the other and reached out to shake his hand.

Thomas extended his hand and said, "It is wonderful to finally meet you, Mrs. Frisch."

"Oh, well, do come in." The foursome shifted and organized themselves awkwardly, the way people do when they've just met and questions are begging to be asked.

"So, Rachel tells us you worked for the Rendell administration. You know, he was Jewish, don't you?" her mother said.

Oh no, here it comes, Rachel thought. The Jewish theme already.

"Yes, as a matter of fact, I would like to see him become the first Jewish president of the United States."

"Oh, wouldn't that be a miracle? It'll never happen in my lifetime. Americans would sooner elect Arnold Schwarzenegger, an Austrian, than a Jew. I still have to pinch myself when I think the Terminator is running Calyfornia," her mother said mocking Arnold's thick Austrian accent.

"No kidding. When I first heard he was running, I thought my friends were playing a joke on me."

"When I first heard it, I thought I was having a senior moment. Like when my mother with advanced Alzheimer's saw Reagan on the cover of *Time* magazine. She said, 'What's he doing on the cover? He's a B-rate movie actor.'" Thomas laughed a deep, hearty laugh. Rachel followed suit anxiously.

"Mrs. Frisch, now that we have an African American president, will a Jewish or female president be next?" The foursome pushed out forced laughter in unison.

"I'd put my money on a woman."

"How about some wine?" Rachel suggested. "Do we have any Californian pinot noir? It's Thomas's favorite." Rachel whisked her mom away to the wine cellar to divert any more potentially controversial subject threads, such as race or religion or—God forbid—their relationship status.

As soon as they were out of earshot her mother frowned. "Why didn't you tell us, Rachel? Talk about putting us on the spot. You probably did this on purpose, so you wouldn't get an earful. But hopefully, he's just transitional."

"Transitioning from what to what? From someone I like to someone you like?"

"From someone less suitable to someone more suitable."

"To someone Jewish, you mean."

"Or Anglo."

"In a matter of minutes, you've expanded the acceptable dating pool from Jews to white men?"

"Mulatto children have such a difficult life."

"Who said anything about children?"

"I just think it would be easier all around for you to marry a Jew."

"Easier for you, you mean."

"I want what's best for you."

"You mean, you want what's best for you to be what's best for me. What's best for me is Thomas."

"You're doing this to hurt us, aren't you?"

"God, Mom. Why would I choose someone just to hurt you?"

"All I ever wanted was…"

"This isn't about you. For once in your life, can't you see that? Thomas is the first man I've ever really loved."

Her mother scurried into the back of the wine cellar. Rachel started to wonder if she would emerge again before the evening was over. She called out to Rachel, "What kind of wine did you say Thomas liked?"

"California pinot noir." Rachel could hear her mother picking up bottles, looking at them, and then placing them back into their slots. Clink, silence, clatter. She must have considered a dozen bottles before finally selecting one. She reemerged with two bottles and held them up for Rachel to see. Rachel nodded, but she didn't know anything about wine, except for general categories, like merlot, pinot noir, and cabernet sauvignon. They ascended from the darkness without speaking.

Her mother presented the two bottles to Thomas, announcing, "Kistler Cuvee Catherine Vineyard Russian River 2002 and 1992."

"Excellent," said Thomas. He smiled at Rachel. "Pinot noir is my favorite variety—even though it's a fickle grape. It's sexy but temperamental and can be an unpredictable performer: it's difficult to grow, and is finicky about the climate it's grown in."

"Yes. A fickle grape, indeed," said her mother. "My favorite pinots come from the regions around Santa Barbara and the Russian River." Her mother opened the 2002 bottle. She handed the cork to Thomas, who smelled it and nodded with approval. She poured his glass and waited for his reaction. He sipped, swished, and swallowed.

"Sublime, Mrs. Frisch." His reaction dismantled her wrinkled brow expression, but her mouth was frozen in a drooping half-moon shape, the disapproving look Rachel saw every time she brought a non-Jewish boyfriend home.

Rachel felt an urgent need to escape, her blood still boiling from the cellar talk. With a tilt of her head toward the stairs, Rachel summoned Thomas upstairs to her childhood bedroom as Mrs. Frisch walked back into the kitchen to finish her dinner preparations.

"Are you okay, Rach? You seem tense. Your parents are charming."

"Yeah, you should have seen the charming scene down in the wine cellar. My mom is freaked out about us. This is going to be a long evening."

"She must not be that freaked. That pinot goes for $300 and $400 a pop."

"What? You're kidding."

"Nope, it's top of the line."

Rachel's eyes widened with astonishment. Her mother didn't part with her high-end bottles of wine easily. They only made their appearance on very special occasions, such as engagements, bar mitzvahs, and anniversaries. Then it crossed her mind that this was not so much a celebratory moment as a test to see if Thomas really knew his wine. If he didn't, it would be one more strike against him and would seal the deal for her mother.

Rachel took Thomas's hand and together they descended the steps. Rachel held her breath for the next hurdle.

The pair reentered the dining room as her mother filled the wine glasses with the 1992 vintage, the higher-end bottle. Thomas took the chair next to Mrs. Frisch.

Enough with the wine-tasting rituals. Fill my glass to the rim and let me chug it down. Rachel knew such a gauche action would have horrified her mother; she would have gone running from the dining room and entered one of her weeklong dark bedroom lockdown routines. Instead she said, "Shouldn't we let it breathe?" Rachel glanced at her mother and then Thomas. "That's about all I know about red wine—that it has to breathe."

"Actually, in this case, no." Thomas winked at Mrs. Frisch. "Some older wines become fragile with age and may release their spirit very quickly after the cork is popped."

Rachel reached for her glass, ready for a swig.

"Ah, ah, Rachel. Not until we've had a toast," her mother said with a twinkle in her eye. She was in her element when the focus was on her fine wine collection. Rachel pulled her hand back and shrank into her seat.

"If you had a young wine, you'd want to let it breathe to make up for the oxidation that occurs with fine wines as they age in the cellar. When it comes to wine, there's no substitute for aging," Thomas explained as his eyes caught the sparkle of the liquid grapes in the crystal glasses.

Her mother glanced at Thomas and filled his glass half full, twisting the bottle so as not to lose a drop. He grasped the stem of the glass with his long fingers and held it up to the light to admire its ruby red color. He then swirled the wine in the glass to release the aroma.

"Go ahead, Thomas, give it a try." Her mother clearly couldn't wait until the toast to have someone sample one of the premiere bottles from her collection—even if it was another one of Rachel's poor boyfriend choices. Thomas swirled the wine once more, sniffed its bouquet, and took a sip. He then took a slightly larger sip and aerated the wine in his mouth, making a slight slurping sound. Thomas closed his eyes and sat in silence, his fingers still wrapped around the stem. Rachel looked at her mother out of the corner of her eye. She was literally on the edge of her seat.

"So, what do you think?" asked her mother.

Here comes the test.

Thomas opened his eyes and said, "Soft, velvety, with a superb richness and depth. Like liquid silk."

Her mother's face released its protest scowl and beamed. She leaned toward Thomas and touched his shoulder. "What did you detect?"

"Red berries and violets. A brilliant finish."

"Don't you think that once you've tasted a great pinot you're hooked for life?"

Rachel could have sworn her mother nearly clapped in glee. She rolled her eyes, embarrassed by her mother's giddiness over the wine tasting with Thomas. No one noticed.

For once, Rachel didn't care that she felt invisible. She started to believe that she wouldn't have to make an impossible choice.

Defying Gravity

Most people run away with the circus, but Zoe ran away from it. Not because of creepy clowns or unsavory ringmasters. No, not because of that.

When Zoe auditioned for Bartholomew Barkley III, a man with sprouting hair, beady eyes, and a bulbous nose, she scrambled up satiny, red strands of cloth. She wrapped herself in a piece of silk, disappeared as if in a cocoon, and then reappeared, having twisted one strand around her ankle. Zoe threw her petite body into a swirling freefall, and caught herself at the last minute with the loop around her ankle. She then looped both strands around her legs and arched backwards to catch the fabric in a flying backbend, twirling all the while. Zoe fell into splits, straddled between the strands. She slid the silk around her waist and, as the fabric unraveled, twirled to the ground. Zoe curtsied to BB III, all one hundred pounds of her. As she dipped, her chocolate-cherry ringlets bounced every which way, and her dimples parenthetically set off her slightly off-kilter smile. Her wide grin looked as if it had been misplaced—a Mrs. Potato Head smile on a Tater Tot face. Zoe's sunken eyes looked sullen even when she smiled. Her face was a work in contrasts. Big, small; happy, sad; crooked, straight.

To BB III, she looked as if she were barely of age, making love to the cloth, becoming enveloped in it, straddling, twisting, and embracing it. BB III was sure this would be a crowd pleaser for the gents. He featured big animals for the kids, cute little animals for the ladies, and now an adolescent cloth dancer for his male audience.

BB III watched, mesmerized—having never seen an aerialist so talented—although he would never admit this to her in her short stint with the circus. He made a point of keeping his performers guessing for fear of them running off with the Froggy Circus, his term of derision for Cirque de Soleil.

With a flat affect, BB III said, "Thank you Miss Jacobsen. We'll review your video in committee and give you a call sometime in the next few weeks if we're interested. Otherwise, you won't hear from us." She left, unsure of the competition she faced, unsure of his reaction, unsure even of her talent.

He phoned that night—only hours after her audition—and invited her to join the Barkley Brothers Circus. She celebrated in silk in her parent's back yard by performing a stunt no aerialist in history had ever been able to do. Only the night crawlers and prowlers witnessed this monumental feat. It would become a regular part of her act.

A month after joining the circus, Zoe was awakened before dawn in her trailer by a relentless clanking sound. Her subconscious had incorporated it into her dream state by conjuring up a chain gang of circus clowns in prison stripes working on a railroad. Moments of silence were punctuated by the sound of a heavy object crashing against a trailer wall and reverberating through the circus camp. She tried to tune it out by pulling a pillow over her head, but the metallic crashes stalked her. Zoe threw on her sweats and emerged from the trailer, heading toward the clanking sound emanating from the animal cages. The black curtain of night was drawing up, casting faint hues on the black-and-white world. Trailer lights sparkled in the darkness and created a surreal aura in the temporary world of the traveling circus.

Zoe discovered one of the elephants, the smallest of the bunch, slamming her trunk against the cage door as if trying to free herself from captivity. The others were either standing motionless or meandering around the dirt-floored cage in a daze.

Zoe approached the agitated elephant and called out to her, "Enough already! I'm trying to get some sleep. We all have to perform today, and you're not helping things with your racket. Take a chill pill. Will you?"

The elephant paused, swaying her giant ears and trunk to gaze at Zoe. She blinked several times, slid her trunk into her mouth and swung it out again. Then she moved her head back, swinging her trunk out in front of her and focused on Zoe again, blinking in slow motion. She noticed large beads of sweat cascading down the creature's wrinkled face. Zoe could have sworn the elephant was trying to make sense of her message and communicate something. An eerie feeling swept over her, as if she and the elephant had an understanding. Not possible, Zoe thought as she scurried out of the pungent animal cages toward her trailer. The scent was that of an overheated hamster cage.

At 4:30 a.m., it was still too early for the circus performers and trainers to be stirring in their trailers, but Zoe knew getting back to sleep wasn't in the cards. She brewed herself a fresh cup of French roast and sat on her trailer steps, warming her hands on her mug, wondering what had just happened.

Three weeks and five cities later in St. Louis, there was word that protesters from People for the Ethical Treatment of Animals (PETA) were swarming in front of the circus entrance with their creepy circus-master masks, bloody elephant costumes, photos of mistreated circus animals circa 1900s and protest signs, pestering circus goers. Among the signs displayed was one that read: *Barkley Brothers Abuses Animals: Ask Us—We Worked There.*

For God's sake, let the children enjoy the circus the way I did, Zoe wanted to say to the meddling protesters. Why everything in modern life had become a political issue, she didn't understand. The world had become far too politicized and had lost its sense of wonder, joy, and playfulness. People were claiming abuse at every turn—from school playgrounds where children weren't allowed to touch each other anymore to circuses, where kids couldn't enjoy animals without the accusations of animal rights protesters.

To quell the protests, the elephant act was preceded by a video explaining that the elephants were treated humanely and given proper care and attention.

Zoe knew, because the ringmaster and owners made it perfectly clear, that traditional circuses were at risk of going under if they lost their big animal acts, so critical were the tigers and elephants to the fiscal health of the circuses. Zoe's dream—to run away with the circus—was being realized, and she felt that the animal rights people would eventually snatch it away.

She was tempted to give the protesters a piece of her mind, but circus policy prohibited performers from interacting with protesters. Only the public relations professionals were allowed to speak on behalf of the circus after being thoroughly briefed by their legal counsel.

During opening night in Denver, Zoe counted only five elephants as she clung to her silk at the top of the tent. Jujube was missing. After performing and bowing in every direction to thunderous applause, Zoe made her way to the animal cages to check on her.

As she approached, she heard a whacking sound that increased in tempo and force. She couldn't believe her eyes. The head animal trainer was using chains to whip Jujube's legs and behind. Her front and hind legs were chained to a pole so she couldn't move away from the beatings. The trainer was viciously attacking, yelling at, cursing, and shocking the elephant. Jujube was emitting agonizing screams while recoiling from the assaults. The trainer then struck the elephant with a bullhook, sunk it into her flesh and twisted it back and forth until she screamed in pain. Zoe switched her cell phone to video and taped the torture session.

Then she hid behind the big-cat cages until the coast was clear. She leaned into the elephant cage and spoke to Jujube, trying to figure out how to free her from the shackles.

"Jujube, sweetie, I'm so, so sorry," Zoe called out.

"What are you doing here? Performers are not permitted back here during off hours," scolded a harsh booming voice. Zoe was startled. She thought she was alone with Jujube.

"A better question would be—what were you doing to her? Is the video we show every night to thousands of people about the humane treatment of elephants a lie?" Zoe shouted.

"Trust me. These are just standard operating procedures for a circus." The trainer walked over and summoned her to the exit.

"You call whipping the living daylights out of an animal standard operating procedures?" Zoe didn't budge.

"It's in her best interest. She has to learn how to perform. Otherwise, she'll be sent away. Now listen, you need to leave right now."

"Where would she be sent?" Zoe asked.
"Wherever. A zoo, where life is no better than here. Believe me."

"Anything is better than this. Maybe those PETA people are right."

"Do yourself a favor. If you ever so much as mention PETA to the owners or ringmaster, you'll be history," said the trainer.

"At least remove those chains. Let her roam free in her cage," Zoe pleaded.

The trainer, who had no response to her plea, practically shoved her away from the elephant cage. Zoe saw that this man was an expert in forcing creatures to go against their wills.

She watched as he moved from the elephant cage to the lion cage. The doors connecting the cages weren't locked. Although Zoe didn't know it then, this data collection would soon be critical to Jujube.

Each night during the elephant act, Zoe would climb the red silk, hand over hand, satiny strand between her legs, to the top of the tent and wait. From this vantage point, she watched Mango, Kiwi, Papaya, Dwarf, Paw Paw, Kaki, and Jujube wow the crowd with their soccer skills. They juggled, kicked, and tossed the ball with their trunks. With each trick, the collective "oohs and ahs" of the crowd wafted to the top of the tent and were absorbed by Zoe. Thus she knew the importance of the elephants to the survival of the circus. As much as she liked to believe it was she who was the greatest show on earth, she knew she played second fiddle to the magnificent pachyderms.

Her act began after the elephant finale when they were made to squat on portable toilets and look like they were taking a shit. Sound effects of farting and dropping giant loads wafted through the air and the crowd roared in delight. In Wichita, twenty-five performances after her first, she felt sickened by the elephant humiliation. When the crimson spotlights shone on her tiny body wrapped in red silk, she froze in rage and refused to perform. The tango music lilted while the lights—magenta, violet, indigo, and crimson— danced around her still figure. She could sense the crowd's apprehension and fear that something was terribly wrong. The lighting technician quickly shifted the beams to the floor and the Russians on horses were cued with "Theme from the Bolsheviks." As the horses galloped in with the Russians standing on and slipping and flipping off the sides of the horses, Zoe slid down to the dirt floor of the circus tent, hardly noticed, except by one person.

After the show, Rupert, the ringmaster, barged into her dressing room, unannounced. He wore his bleached blonde toupee, tight red cummerbund with matching bowtie, and extra-tight leggings with an unnecessary dance cup accentuating his bulge. Rupert clutched a whip, and she could have sworn he was about to use it on her. His face was as red as his bowtie.

"What in God's name happened up there, Zoe? What the *hell* were you thinking? That doesn't happen in my circus. You pull one more of those and you're a goner! Do you understand me?" Then he cracked his whip in the air. "I'm not leaving until you tell me what happened." He stood over her, stroking the leather whip with his chubby fingers.

"I don't like the pooping elephant routine. It's offensive."

"Well, if you were the artistic director, we'd have something to discuss. But you're just a pole dancer." He chuckled to himself.

"Aerialist."

"Whatever."

"The toilet act is demeaning. Would you do it—shit on the toilet in front of thousands of people?"

"No, but the clowns would and have."

"The clowns have a choice. The elephants don't."

"Next time I want artistic direction from you, little miss upstart, I'll ask you. Until then, just climb your rope, put out, and shut up." Rupert and his whip exited.

"It's silk," she called after him and then added, "you moron."

As Zoe returned to her trailer after hanging out with the trapeze artist, she noticed that her trailer door was cracked open. *Strange, I thought I closed my door.* She whipped out her Swiss army knife—not the best defense, but better than nothing.

As she pushed open the door, with her pocket knife leading the way, she was startled by a man's silhouette. "Who are you and what are you doing in my trailer?" Zoe demanded.

"It's circus policy that if we suspect a performer is compromising circus security, we have the authority to investigate without prior authorization," said Mr. Barkley in his most official voice.

She dropped her knife-holding hand by her side, but didn't fold the knife into its base. "On the outside, this is called breaking and entering, Mr. Barkley. But apparently, we don't always adhere to the laws on the outside. And exactly what are you investigating?"

"I'm not at liberty to say. It would compromise circus security."

"Oh, right. Is the circus infiltrated with spies in clown costumes? Or are there trade secrets about how to torture the animals for the best performance results?"

He stood in the middle of her trailer like a ringmaster taking control of the rings. "Listen, I hear you were witness to an elephant beating. You must understand that the trainer has been suspended without pay. Do you know that what you saw is not tolerated by this circus? You will not speak a word of this to anyone. Is that clear? If this leaks to the press, I'll know the source. Let's just say I'll see to it that you never perform again in any circus."

"Are you threatening me?" Zoe asked.

"It's not a threat; it's a promise," he replied with his brows knit together and his mouth a straight line.

"Well, you might rethink your threat when you see this." Zoe displayed the elephant beating video on her phone.

He watched for a few seconds as the animal trainer used a bullhook on Jujube. His posture stiffened and his face tightened. It almost looked as though he would lunge for the phone, but he stopped himself. "For a little thing, you sure are a menace. Listen, I must see significant improvements in your upholding the Barkley Brothers' promise or you and your silk threads will walk. Do you understand me?" Mr. Barkley ducked out of her trailer and slammed the door, shaking her compact circus home.

Zoe knew that she had passed the point of no return with Mr. Barkley, but she also had a sense that he would keep her around long enough to confiscate her cell phone with the damning evidence and then cut her loose.

Instead of going to bed, Zoe hopped on her computer and formulated a plan. It was a half-baked plan with good intentions, the kind that only the young are capable of. Zoe's plan was driven by compassion and impulsivity and the belief that morality was on her side—a combination that may be fatally flawed, unless the wings of providence swoop in and carry the plan to safety.

She could have involved lawyers, committees, investigations, and hearings, but she was too impatient for all that. Adults took too damned long to make things happen. By then, Jujube would be another broken spirit in an elephant hull.

Zoe stayed up all night mapping, plotting, diagramming, and calculating. Math wasn't her strong suit, but whimsical dreams were. Despite this, she hatched what she thought was a clever plan. During the early morning hours when the animals were stirring and the carnies were snoozing, she had delusions of becoming a sleuth or a private eye or even a cross between Spider Woman and Bat Girl—scaling buildings and catapulting herself into inaccessible places, in spandex, of course.

There was no time to waste.

The following day after her performance, she packed up her cherished items, laptop, and aerial equipment. She had a close call when one of her clown friends rushed in and asked with a yuk-yuk if she was running away from the circus.

"Oh, no, just getting organized. You know me—in a perpetual state of chaos."

Her heart beat out of her little bird-cage chest as she shooed him, his orange clown afro, and big red nose out of her trailer.

"You sure know how to make a clown cry," he said.

Zoe made a run for it, with her backpack and aerial gear, as soon as the last trailer light was extinguished. Lucky for her mission that the tents were illuminated from the outside to create a starry, starry night effect for passersby and circus enthusiasts.

The trickiest part of her plan was to climb up a cable that spanned the entire height of the animal tent. But having scaled everything from poles to fabrics to ropes, Zoe felt confident that she could make it to the top. Before mounting the cable, she slipped on trapeze gloves with gripping material. Then, like an upside down tightrope walker, she inched her way up the cable to the apex of the tent. Playing to crowds of thousands was never as nerve-wracking as this. She felt wobbly, shaky, and unstable. "Noodle knees," they called it in the circus biz—something she hadn't felt since circus arts school.

At the apex of the tent, she gripped the tip and peeked into its small opening. Zoe would have to secure her rigging to the outside of the tent. She clipped her carabineers to two opposing cables. Normally rigging should be more extensive, but she would have to forgo a secure setup for a makeshift one. In circus arts school, the instructors warned aerialists to never, ever cut corners when rigging.

Like a seamstress threading a needle, she poked the fabric through the slight opening at the top of the tent. She watched it cascade down to the…lions! She would have to lower herself into a den of lions to get to the elephants. She hadn't figured lion taming into her plan.

Zoe popped her head through the top like a malfunctioning jack-in-the box and saw that the elephants were catty-corner from the lions. If she could get past the lions, she knew that the cages were conjoined without locks.

Had she had a tremulous nature, Zoe would not have attempted the elephant heist through the lion's den. But cowardly girls don't join the circus as aerialists. Performing death-defying feats was her specialty. As Zoe slithered down the fabric, she kept her eyes peeled on the lions. A lioness in the corner had spotted her and had started to pace. Zoe wrapped herself up in the fabric cocoon—attempting to give the impression that she was a giant red creature towering over the restless feline. In her cocoon with a tiny peep hole, she descended the rest of the way. The feline was frozen with the look of a curious but crotchety old man. When Zoe's feet touched the earth, she whispered to the lion in a comforting tone, the way she used to talk to Nani, her family cat. She crept sideways toward the cage door—never turning her back on the lion. The lion moved toward her, and as panic seized Zoe's arms and legs, the lion opened her mouth and released a giant, toothy, tongue-protruding yawn. "Oh, I don't scare you; I bore you. That's good. That's very, very good," she said, waves of relief relaxing her taut limbs. The bored feline plopped down and rested her giant head on her paws.

Zoe clicked open the cage door handle, walked through a hall that led directly to the elephants' back entrance. Pausing to breathe a sigh of relief over not becoming kitty chow, she didn't worry that her plan would fail or that a circus top dog might be on her trail. Nor did she think about the strands of fabric flapping in the lion's cage—evidence more damning than fingerprints.

Zoe led Jujube down crisscrossing roads to the highway. After two hours of cajoling, the pair finally reached the highway at 3:20 a.m. Zoe was now intimately familiar with the meaning of "lumbering elephant." To move Jujube along, she bribed her with bananas, mangos, and apples she had pilfered from the circus cafeteria.

The main road was a long stretch of deserted highway. Occasionally trucks would pass, but didn't spot Zoe and Jujube in the shadows. Holding Jujube's trunk, Zoe guided her to the other side of the highway and stood there, thinking about the thrill she was about to give weary truckers. She hadn't thought of what might happen if law enforcement officials found her or had she considered the trouble she'd be in for stealing circus property.

Thirty minutes had passed before she spotted a dim light in the distance. She stuck her thumb out, although she was well aware that her thumb would be upstaged by a hitchhiking elephant. The headlights brightened as the car approached and then whizzed past. It was a sports car doing at least 100 mph. Several minutes later, she saw a truck illuminated with cab lights. She hoped it might be big enough to fit Jujube, who was now fidgety. A fidgety elephant was a bit problematic, Zoe discovered. And she had nothing else to bribe her with. Jujube had depleted Zoe's backpack full of fruit in just two hours.

"Jujube, hold still," she pleaded as the truck flashed its high beams and then slowed to a stop next to her.

"Well, God damn! God damn! Darlin', I was clearing the angel dust from my eyes back there and then shaking myself awake, thinking I had done near started to doze. Am I hallucinatin' or is that an elephant you got there, little missy?" shouted the trucker, with his arm resting on the side of his cab.

"Sir, you're not hallucinating. It is indeed an elephant. Her name is Jujube."

"And my name is Billy Ray. Are you two runnin' away from home or somethin'?"

"Oh no, sir."

"For Lord's sake, don't tell me she's your pet. Jeez, people are going off the deep end with pets these days. Back when I was young, folks were just fine with puppies and kittens. These days people have to have exotics—snakes, giant lizards, and now, now…Jiminy Cricket, elephants."

"She's not my pet, sir."

"Well pardon me for pryin', but why are you hitchhikin' with an elephant at this ungodly hour? It ain't normal for a girl to hitchhike at all, let alone with an elephant, you know."

Zoe looked up at Jujube and then back at Billy Ray. "Got enough room in there for an elephant?"

Billy Ray was so tickled by her question, he slammed the side of his truck with his palm and let out a yelp that startled Jujube. When he got a hold of himself and quelled the laughing aftershocks that sounded like hootin' and hollerin' with a lid on them, he said, "Sorry little missy, I don't mean to offend, but this takes the cake for strange situations on the road, you know?" Then like a kid trying not to laugh in class, he pinched his nose and asked, "Where you headed?"

"Hohenwald, Tennessee."

"What's down there?"

"Elephant sanctuary."

"You mean like a place where elephants can pray?"

"Something like that," Zoe said, thinking this could be a hard sell.

"Is this an elephant rescue or somethin'?" He gave Zoe a knowing wink and smiled a pumpkin smile. Billy Ray seemed so proud of his inference that he appeared ready and willing to be an accomplice. "'Fraid I'm headed in the wrong direction. Let me see if I can get my buddy who's trailin' me by thirty minutes. Hold your horses, er elephants." His hootin' and hollerin' threatened to resurface after his little funny, but he swallowed so hard his Adam's apple bobbed down and up, and his hysterics went down his gullet.

Billy Ray called his friend and discovered that highway patrol cars were on the trail of a hit-and-run.

"Well, I'll be damned. He says the highway patrol are comin'. We've gotta hide you and your friend, missy. Otherwise, they'll pick you up for hitchhikin,' and I'm not

123

sure what the charge would be for the elephant. That's one they probably don't have in their books. Woo-wee! If this ain't the wildest night I've had in the last twenty-five years on the road!"

The only problem was that Jujube didn't want to cooperate with the plan.

"Don't they say, stubborn as an elephant?" Billy Ray said as they pushed Jujube's behind in tandem, to no avail. Two hundred ninety pounds of humans pushing seven-thousand pounds of elephant. Zoe had failed to include this in her calculations.

"I think it's stubborn as a mule," said Zoe. "C'mon Jujube. C'mon," Zoe urged the elephant as she attempted to guide her into the tractor-trailer. "Scoot!"

"We can scare the bejesus out of her."

"No, I don't want to do that."

"It's either that or…Those highway patrolmen will be comin' along before you can say jack rabbit or, in this case, Jujube elephant." He was clearly having the time of his life. Zoe was certain that hiding an elephant beat endless stretches of open highway and cornfields any day. Cornfields!

"Hey, I think I know something that will work. Can you go grab some corn over there?" She pointed to the cornfield. "Maybe we'll lure her in with corn."

Sure enough, Billy Ray and Zoe moved seven-thousand pounds of elephant with two kilos of corn. He lowered the automated tractor-trailer door and told Zoe to get into his cab and duck.

"Don't want the fuzz to think there's any monkey business goin' on. Little do they know there's elephant business." He was in hysterics about his joke. Zoe faked a laugh for good measure. After all, he was her accomplice in the elephant caper.

A few minutes later, the state troopers pulled up to Billy Ray's tractor-trailer. The troopers with wide-brimmed hats and stiff posture appeared from behind the tinted power window.

"Everything okay in there?" shouted the passenger-side trooper.

"A-OK, sirs! Couldn't be better!" answered Billy Ray with an A-OK sign to match.

"You're not having any trouble with your cab?" asked the trooper.

"Nope, she's runnin' like a champ." At the "p" in champ, Jujube kicked the trailer wall so hard, the truck shimmied. The state troopers did a well-choreographed double take.

"You got a horse in there or something? You wouldn't be following regulations if that were the case," said the trooper behind the wheel. "Gotta be traveling with a regulation trailer. I'm afraid we'd have to give you a citation and a hefty fine for that."

"No, sir, the cargo shifts from time to time. That's all," said Billy Ray without hesitation.

"Might want to secure it before too long," said the passenger-side trooper, stating the obvious. Jujube kicked again, with greater force.

In her crunched and ducked position, Zoe felt like an appendage to her pounding heart. She scrunched her eyes, shook her head, and begged Jujube to stop.

"Well, I'll be. You sure called it. I'll be spendin' some time securin' my cargo at the next truck stop. She'll be tight as a drum," said Billy Ray. Zoe had to hand it to her accomplice; he was smooth and polished with the law. Some people's super heroes were suave muscle men swooping down in capes; hers was now officially a hillbilly trucker.

The patrolmen conferred for a few minutes, their stiff hats tilting and straightening as they fiddled with their overly equipped uniforms and squad car. Ten minutes after stopping to check on Billy Ray's truck, the troopers flipped on the red, white, and blue flashers. Nothing quite as patriotic as enforcing the law.

Zoe's sigh of relief ricocheted back into her throat and became a lump she couldn't swallow. If she hadn't known any better, she would have thought that her heart had come unhinged and had relocated to her head.

The passenger-side officer got out. "We're going to need to take a look for ourselves, mister. I can smell it when something ain't right. Get out of your cab, hands in the air. Is there anyone else in the truck with you?"

Billy Ray didn't really know how to answer that. There were two someone elses—a runaway girl and her storybook pet. He wasn't sure, though, if elephants counted as someone or something.

"Sir, answer the question or I'll have to search the entirety of the truck."

Billy Ray shot Zoe a what-the-hell-do-we-do-now glance, and said, "Yes, there's someone else. She'll be right out." He motioned with his startled eyeballs for her to come out of hiding. Then he jumped out of the cab with his hands up— panicked on the inside, calm on the outside. He took his time opening the tractor-trailer, while he wracked his brain to come up with a good story. His lame brain wasn't producing anything worth a can of beans. As he threw open the door, the patrolman's face lit up like a little boy's at a circus.

"Well, I'll be damned. My name ain't Gus if that's not an elephant. That there is a real-life honest-to-goodness elephant!" He repeated the words for his disbelieving eyes and radioed his partner that he had to come see "the cargo" for himself. When he said "cargo," he let out an ironic snort.

The other state trooper raced around the cab, ready to assist his partner in this all-important mission, looked up, and said, "Jesus H. Christ, it's an elephant! Gus, what do you know; it's a god-damned elephant!"

Bud, now trying his best to maintain a modicum of law-enforcement composure, said, "What are your plans concerning this elephant? I don't s'pose you're the rightful owner now. Are you? You two with the circus or something?"

Billy Ray did some fast talking. "Yes, indeedy, this beaut sure is mine. We keep her down on the farm for hauling crops, hay, and such. Best dern farm animal we've ever had. Better than a horse, donkey, and a mule rolled into one."

"A farm elephant. That's a new one, ain't it, Gus?"

"Why you hauling her around in your eighteen-wheeler?" asked Gus.

"That's a fair question, sir. Well, it's a sad story, really. You see she's got some kind of serious condition with her trunk—clogged hose or something—and ain't no vet in these parts can do elephant plumbing, as you can imagine. A clogged hose on an elephant is like having plumbin', eatin', and grippin' problems all rolled into one. You can just imagine the severity of that. So we have to take her to a special clinic down south."

"Where's that at?" asked Gus.

"Tennessee. Closest vet specializing in unclogging elephant trunks."

The patrolmen were stymied, unsure of their next move. Then Bud said, "Gus, what are the regulations concernin' the transporting of elephants?"

Despite his attempts to be a law enforcement man in charge, Gus looked at Bud and let out an explosive guffaw. He threw his head back and laughed the uncontrollable laugh of a man who normally kept his laughter under lock and key.

Bud puffed up his chest and tightened his arms flexed over his gun belt. He shot Gus a reprimanding glare and shook his head at the unprofessionalism of his partner. But as Gus's laughter spiraled out of control, Bud couldn't hold back any longer and released a belly laugh that could've been heard on the west side of Kansas.

There they were—elephant thief, accomplice, and uproarious law enforcement officers, all peering up at an elephant's rump, contemplating The Elephant Problem.

Keeping score in her head with each action and reaction, Zoe saw this as a very positive development in the elephant caper. As she had learned from her stint with the circus, entertained folks are happy folks—more lenient and forgiving. She waited for their next move.

"Listen, here, what did you say your name was—Billy Ray?" Gus asked.

"Yes, sir."

"And who's this here little lady you got with you?" Gus winked at Zoe.

"That's Sarah Jane, my youngest." Zoe dipped into an abbreviated curtsied to play along.

"Cutie pie—that one. Gonna be a heartbreaker." Gus eyed Zoe up and down and up again.

Eyeballing was part of a state trooper's job perks, Zoe figured. If she didn't have an elephant rescue underway, she might have shot him a get-your-eyeballs-off-my-body look. Instead she struck a coy pose—biting her lip and casting her gaze downward.

"Already is, sir. Already is," said Billy Ray, with a forlorn look on his face, shaking his head for effect.

"Bud and I have decided," although Bud hadn't decided a thing, "that we'll have to issue a citation for improper elephant transport procedures. It'll be a $600 fine. Once you get her to where she's goin', and get her trunk unclogged and all that, you'll have to make sure that you follow appropriate rules and regulations upon her return. If you don't, we'll issue a warrant for your arrest for illegal elephant activities. Is that clear?"

"Yes, sir. I'll make sure it's by the letter of the law." He winked at Zoe, who had started breathing again.

Gus wrote up a ticket and handed it to Billy Ray, "Alright, drive safe now and good luck with your elephant plumbing problem." As the state troopers walked off, Zoe heard Bud say, "Elephant transport procedures?" Gus and Bud broke out in hysterics again.

Zoe had never seen such jolly state troopers in her life. She started to believe that Jujube was a talisman.

Four states, five truck stops, ten pit stops, seven kilos of corn, four hamburgers, and three six-packs of Coca Cola got Zoe and Billy Ray to Hohenwald, Tennessee. As they drove past the sanctuary gates, Zoe's eyes rested on the expanse of lush pastureland and barns.

"Well, now what?" asked Billy Ray.

Zoe's plan ended at: arrive at the elephant sanctuary. "Um, I guess just let her out."

"I doubt they just want people dropping off random elephants," noted Billy Ray.

"I'm guessing it probably doesn't happen too often."

"No, Sarah Jane, you've got that right," he said. He had taken to calling her Sarah Jane after the state trooper incident, and added that he wanted to adopt her. She thanked Billy Ray kindly, but told him her father position was already filled.

As they were deciding what to do next, a woman with blonde pigtails, high color, and dirty overalls was approaching the truck with a stern expression and her arms in a stop-go-back position. "Can I help you?" she called up to Zoe and Billy Ray. "Who are you? Unauthorized vehicles are not allowed on this property. You must leave the premises immediately," she ordered as she pointed toward the exit gate.

Zoe leaned out of the truck window and shouted down to her. "I've, well, we've rescued an elephant named Jujube from the Barkley Brothers Circus, and I was hoping you'd provide a home to her. She's a young one."

The pigtailed woman's stern face softened and she extended her arms, beckoning Zoe out of the truck. Zoe obliged and jumped down. From military guard to nurturing earth mama in a matter of seconds, the woman gave Zoe an extended hug—longer than Zoe's closest friends or relatives would ever embrace her. As she pushed Zoe back to take a look at her, she said, "Call me Ellie, short for, what else, elephant! Bless you, child. Bless you." She put her arm around Zoe and guided her to the back of the truck, as if it were pre-orchestrated for Ellie to take the plan from here. "I assume our angel is back here." She laughed. "Silly me, where else would she be?"

Zoe called Billy Ray and asked him to open the trailer.

"Dear, dear, dear. Sweet Jujube. How long have you had her on the road?"

"16 hours."

"Oh my. Poor dear. I'll bet she's famished." Billy Ray pried open the door and Jujube's tail end was exposed. "Oh, she's a beauty!"

Zoe looked up at Jujube's behind, puzzled and said, "Um, how can you tell?"

"Listen; she's in good shape compared to most. We get them after they've suffered years and years of abuse. You've done a great thing—the best years of her life are ahead of her. The others will adore her." Ellie's pigtails bobbed as she bounced up and down on her tiptoes.

Zoe wondered if spending so much time with elephants made a person a little kooky.

"So, she's a female—right?"

"Yes, why?"

"Oh, thank goddess." Ellie put her hands together in prayer. "We only take female elephants."

"Really? Why?"

"Because it isn't natural for adult female and male Asian elephants to live together. Asian elephants are matriarchal by nature; they live in herds of related females and only very young males. Now if humans could just learn from elephants, we'd be better off. Don't you think?"

As Ellie maneuvered Jujube out of the truck, Zoe noticed a nearby elephant that looked as though she were holding a paintbrush with her trunk and painting on a giant canvas secured to a tree.

"Ellie, what is that elephant doing?" Zoe asked as she pointed at the painting elephant.

Without looking over, Ellie replied, "Oh, that's Tempo. She's one of our most accomplished acrylic artists. Once we get Jujube settled, you should go take a look at her work. We display it in our gallery."

Zoe mouthed "wow" but no words came out. This was truly not the circus anymore.

As Ellie nuzzled with, whispered to, and coddled Jujube, she said, "You might be interested to know that Tempo is our most famous elephant. She was in the 1970s show, *Born Free*. Of course, you're too young to remember that show. She was born in Uganda in 1971 and was orphaned because of poachers."

After Ellie made sure that Jujube had enough food and water, she invited Zoe and Billy Ray into the administrative offices for tea and biscuits. Billy Ray declined, saying he'd take a catnap in his cab.

"So is she safe? I mean if the circus comes looking for her?" Zoe asked, munching on a biscuit.

"No, she's not completely safe. Legally, the circus has the right to take her back. And they can press charges against you for stealing their property."

"I don't think they will," said Zoe.

"How can you be so sure?" Ellie asked.

Zoe held up her cell phone and played the video of the elephant beating. "Let's just say this footage—as rough as it is—would look awfully suspicious next to the we-coddle-our-elephants video that they play for the crowd every night."

"Please, please turn that off. I can't bear it," Ellie said as she turned her face away. "So, they know you have this?"

"Yes, Mr. Barkley himself saw it after he broke into my trailer one night." Zoe laughed and continued, "I gave him a private screening of the evidence. In response, he told me if I spilled the beans, he would make sure I never worked in any circus ever again."

"I suppose you're right, then, about the circus not pressing charges or coming after Jujube. Thank God. But are you concerned that he might have the power to blackmail you?"

"Maybe with the traditional circuses, but I doubt he has much clout with Cirque de Soleil. Fortunately, they don't see eye to eye."

As Zoe and Billy Ray left the sanctuary, she saw an elephant wading in a pond, spouting water like an elegant fountain. She dipped her trunk into the pond and trumpeted the water all over her body. On closer inspection, Zoe saw that it was Jujube, wily, muddy and wet. Zoe could have sworn Jujube was smiling at her.

As Elementala was opening in Toronto, Zoe learned that the Barkley Brothers Circus was under investigation for using bullhooks and chaining their elephants. Although she wasn't sure who had been the source of the leak, she was pleased with this development.

Elementala, the newest Cirque de Soleil show, opened with bonfires on stage and smoke wafting up to the top of the tent. Fire dancers and breathers played with, juggled, and swallowed the flames. The show featured the four elements— air, fire, water, and earth.

Fire gave way to air, Zoe's part of the show. Starting in the flames and ascending through smoke, she would slither up a transparent fabric swath to the top of the tent. She looked as if she were dancing on air, arching, swinging, plunging, and twirling while defying gravity. The crowd murmured, yelped, and cheered as she performed. As she descended, air gave way to water. No one seemed to miss the elephants.

Every time Zoe danced on fabric, she imagined Jujube reveling in her pond. Jujube in water, the Barkley Brothers Circus under fire, she in air, and Billy Ray traversing the earth below. Elemental bliss.

Orcinus Pas de Deux

This is going to sound slightly odd, so you'll understand why I guard this secret with my life.

I'm a whale trapped in a woman's body. I know, I know—typically people trapped in others' bodies are the wrong gender, the wrong identity, or living in the wrong era. Even those people are viewed askance. Imagine if I told anyone, especially my adoring hubby, that I'm a whale in a woman's body. They would label me certifiable and commit me to a psych lock-down unit. Not sure what the psych warders would do there: electroshock me back to being human? How would I request that treatment? "I'd like the whale-to-woman ECT, please."

Here's my best guess about what happened. You know how ontogeny recapitulates phylogeny? You're probably thinking, *that's way over my head; dial it back.* Here's the thing. Human embryonic development duplicates the evolutionary stages. When this was occurring in my mom's womb, my embryonic brain froze at the fish stage. Then, although my body continued forming into a human female, my brain went fish all the way.

I know what you science geeks and marine biology aficionados are thinking: whales are not fish. Technically this is correct. But I'm not one to let details hang me up. Whales live in the ocean and stay underwater for long periods of time. So whales are fish-like. That's close enough for me.

The first time I suspected something was when I was subjected to my mom's New Agey humpback whale music. I was into punk rock, so when she first played the harp orca duets, I cringed and tried like hell to tune it out. But that was an impossible feat when I could understand the music. Not the music of the lilting harp, but the song of the whales. At first I thought I was losing it. Psych class had taught me that hearing voices was the hallmark sign of insanity. Hearing whale voices probably made a person extra insane.

When I looked into human-animal communication, I discovered horse whisperers and dog whisperers, bear whisperers and lion whisperers. Why not whale whisperers? After realizing I probably wasn't losing my marbles, I called psychic hotlines for advice. I used my mom's credit card to check with three psychics about speaking whale. Psychic Number 1 repeated, "Blessed be." And said I was blessed to have the gift of talking to animal spirit guides. Psychic Number 2 claimed I was a whale in a past life and should honor that in this life. Psychic Number 3 was convinced I was channeling whales to save them from extinction. I should feel honored that I had been chosen to represent whales to humanity. *Chosen by whom?*

Distraught by all the honors and blessings, especially having the fate of whales rest on my shoulders, I bummed a pack of cigarettes from my mom's loser of a husband, who wouldn't notice his cigs were missing, snuck out my bedroom window in the wintertime wearing nothing but my Miss Piggy PJs. I smoked an entire pack, having never tried smoking before. The next morning, my voice had dropped an octave, so, thinking I was catching a bug, my mom gave me strict orders to stay in bed as she piped "healing" orca music into my room. I stuffed my ears with Kleenex balls and pulled my pillows over my head. I could make out the clicks, whistles, and pulsed calls of mating, feeding, orienting, flirting, calving, and playing. It was clear the composer had edited the vocalization, not understanding whale dialect, but I could still understand the bits and pieces.

Nowhere in orca dialect did I hear messages for hoarding, stealing, or warring, so I concluded their species was light years ahead of ours.

141

I was trapped with my whale-ness. A fish out of water. Like most people who discover something freaky about themselves, I vowed to keep it a secret. Forever.

When I first spotted the ad for a trainer in the Ocean World mag, it was over killer coffee on a chirping spring day. My hubs and I were living in Cinci, convinced it was San Francisco, Midwestern style, so life was good. Of course, it was San Fran sans the Bay, the Victorian architecture, and the charm, but one thing we knew for sure—it was better than Cleveland and way better than Akron.

I froze mid-sip. "Tripper, come here." His nickname was Jack the Tripper derived from his psychedelic college years. When I explained the name to people who shouldn't know the truth, I described Jack as klutzy and two-left-footed, but, in reality, he had been a gifted high-school soccer player. Most people didn't connect the dots, as Tripper was now a sweet, pasty, sedentary accountant, so he looked the part.

"What is it?" he called out, thinking I wanted him to liberate another spider, my one and only fear in life. Well, that and my whale of a secret.

Needless to say, he didn't come.

"Seriously, come here. Now!"

He did that time. "Where is it?"

"It's not a spider. It's something way better." I read aloud, "Ocean World in San Diego seeks a whale trainer. Must be advanced swimmer, some diving and gymnastics preferred. Can you believe it?"

"Believe what?"

"My luck!"

"That ad is your luck?" He didn't want to point out that I knew nothing about tending to large mammals or swimming with massive orca blubber, but I knew he was thinking it. He shot me a worried glance as if my marbles weren't rolling around in our sphere anymore. Then he performed a charade, because he was afraid to say the words aloud. His index finger pointed at the paper, then at me.

I catapulted out of my strawberry-pink ice-cream parlor chair, tumbled my *Hola Cancun!* coffee mug, stained the ad, heaved all one hundred and ninety pounds of him up in the air, and twirled him around until he had vertigo. Generally, the guy is supposed to do that to the girl, but I'm robust, and when I'm animated, my adrenaline enables me to lift cars off of peoples' legs and such. Don't get me wrong. I've never tried it, but I know I could.

"What do you say?" I asked with fisted victory arms, hoping the V would brainwash him into thinking: done deal.

If you knew my husband, you would know what he said. I kid you not. The thing he wanted most in the world was my happiness. Because of this, I believed either most women were whiners about love, or I had won the jackpot.

With each passing day after the diving, swimming, floating, submerging, tumbling audition, I must've heard every second of the clock. I figured I was that many ticks and tocks closer to the call. When it came, I've never felt so close to the second coming.

Only my savior was an eight thousand-pound orca.

We picked up and moved to San Diego, just like that. Tripper's company gave him the green light for a transfer. And, before I knew it, I was in my natural habitat.

My hubby didn't want to interfere with my experience of the second coming, but, being the investigative, cautious sort, he approached me one night as I was curled up on our gently used leather sofa with my five-pound Ocean World training manual.

"I was reading about some orca trainers who have been seriously injured or killed."

I waved him away. "Probably human error. I'm sure if you follow all the procedures, you're good to go, which I'm learning about, Trip. So, don't you worry."

"I mean, they are called *killer* whales after all."

"Misleading. They're actually dolphins. Says so here in my whale, er, dolphin bible."

"Hand me that, Bean." I was Chelsea Bean to him. After I invented Jack the Tripper, he tried to come up with something that rivaled his clever moniker. Chelsea Bean was the best he could do. When I asked him why he chose Bean, he told me that my brown bob reminded him of a coffee bean. My brown bob was a thing of the past, but Bean lived on. He was a numbers guy after all.

"Yes, sir!" I saluted to the sergeant.

As he paged through the binder, he found what he was looking for. "They may be classified as dolphins, Bean, but they aren't Flipper. They can weigh up to nine tons."

I jumped up, grabbed the manual, kissed him on the cheek, and said, "Don't worry. This is going to be a dream come true. And if it's not, Cinci's not going anywhere."

Then he added, "The people filing the lawsuits for these wrongful deaths received millions and signed hush papers."

"Speaking of hushing," I pleaded. And I kissed him to seal the deal.

In making his argument, he was at a disadvantage, of course. What he didn't know was that he was talking to a whale masquerading as a woman.

The Ocean World trainers were astonished by my speedy transition from newbie to seasoned orca trainer. They pried into my background thinking I was holding out on them. "Really, just a high school state champion in fifty-meter butterfly and a little high-platform diving."

Well, that and I'm a whale.

Apparently, I set an Ocean World record from first day to first performance. It was a magical blur of socializing with the orcas, stuffing their gullets with bottomless buckets of fish treats, diving around and below the whales, holding onto fins for dear life, balancing on spouts—first with two noodle legs, then with one, and balancing as the orcas would submerge and surface, diving off their spouts into the pool. A pas de deux with orcas—me, a hundred and twenty-five-pound human, and them an eight-ton whale mass.

A ratio that's a tad off balance. But who's counting?

From drowned rat to mermaid to sea goddess to mini-orca, my evolution was fast and furious. After countless mouthfuls of water, several underwater tricks that left me gasping for breath, and a couple near drownings, I approached Jerry, the aquatic director, on my tiptoes. "Okay, I'm good to go."

Jerry thought I was joking and slapped my shoulder in my wetsuit, "Good one, Chel."

"I'm serious. I'm ready for this weekend's performance."

146

"We don't want to push this."

"We're not. Try me. If it's tragic rather than epic, you can yank me. No hard feelings. Deal?"

"We don't work like that."

"There's always a first." I punched him back.

Although Jerry had turned down my initial offer, he caved because the featured trainer was out with the flu. Jerry was shaking in his water booties. I was floating on air in mine. I don't know if a camera could've captured the action, but I was levitating inches above the slick, fishy deck.

The seals and balls, dolphins and hoops, and synchro swimmers were up first. Then it was debut time for Keiko and me. My shaky, quaky limbs were jolted by the adrenaline pulsing through my body. My grip was secure on Keiko's fins as he torpedoed through the aquamarine pool. I mounted his back and steadied myself, the crowd's roar a backdrop. During the spout diving sequence, it took three takes before I balanced, and dove up and over as he submerged. The crowd was with me every slip of the way. When I resurfaced they gave me a standing O.

If there's heaven on earth, my debut with Keiko was it. That was my Nirvana moment, head in the clouds, heart on fire, water buoying my body, and magic afoot.

I leapt from Keiko to poolside in my black-and-white
orca wetsuit and bowed, extending my arm toward Keiko.
The second time the crowd acknowledged Keiko, I swear he
was smiling. I wanted to run over and squeeze him, but he
dove under and escaped to the holding tanks, away from the
madding crowd.

Jerry ran over and gave me a stiff former-Marine hug.
Although he always threw around Ocean World legalese to
scare me, he liked the fact that I was an impulsive daredevil.
And so did I.

There was one person who didn't, though, and that was
Tripper. He didn't like it one bit. After he presented me with
a dozen two-toned pink tangerine roses in celebration of my
first performance, he cautioned me that it was all moving too
quickly.

"I'm still in one piece. Aren't I?" I said, holding my arms
out and spinning so he could see. I wanted to reveal my
secret to reassure him. The words were there, balanced on the
tip of my tongue. I'm a whale. I'm really a whale! But they
fizzled in my mouth. I'd rather have him worry about my
safety than think I'm a whale of a whacko.

Each time I dove into the orca pool and frolicked with
Keiko, I reminded myself that I was getting paid for this gig. I

never mentioned it to Jerry, but I would have paid him to do this. For the rest of my life.

One morning, Parker, a seasoned trainer, cautioned me that Keiko was thrashing about and biting the other orcas, even making Tilly bleed. This is behavior we had been warned about in training. Occasionally orcas would misbehave like children. It was normal behavior for all orcas—wild or in captivity—to act out. I brushed it off, confident I could soothe him. I slung buckets full of fish, which he gobbled up with glee, and socialized with him poolside. Then without warning, Keiko hurled out of the water, toppling the buckets of fish and ingesting them in one giant gulp. Rather than being alarmed, I was impressed with his feeding ingenuity. He had come to the fish instead of waiting for the fish to come to him.

When I didn't witness any aberrant behavior, I joined him in the pool. I treaded water next to him for several minutes. Keiko imitated me by spyhopping—holding himself partially out of the water. It was as though he was watching me. *What a clever, playful orca!*

Seconds later, a surge of water swept over me and Keiko trapped me underwater. I struggled to swim around him, but he blocked my passage to the surface. I panicked, taking in some water, strategizing ways to outsmart him. I tricked him by diving deep and then zigzagging to the surface. I gasped, clutching the side of the pool. He came after me again, but I flipped my legs up on the side before he could pull me down.

"Keiko, you rascal! What was that?" I admonished him between coughs. Parker and another trainer had hurried over to see if they needed to administer CPR. "I'm fine. Shit, that was a bit unnerving. I think he just wanted to play. Maybe he mistook me for an orca." I said, treading a little too close to the edge of the truth. It was my adrenaline talking.

Parker shook his head and countered with, "More like an appetizer dressed like an orca."

"Oh please." Everyone was getting so touchy about orcas being dangerous animals.

After performances, audience members would cluster around me and request autographed orca posters, blow-up toys, stuffed animals, and t-shirts. I signed their orca memorabilia, Chelsea, the Orca Girrrrl. I was amazed by the amount of Ocean World orca merchandizing—probably worth tens of millions. Little girls and boys with parents in tow would encircle me and say they wanted to grow up to be just like me. Squatting down to their level, I advised them to practice their swimming and diving and to do their homework. I winked at their parents who looked eternally grateful. I could imagine them quoting me. "If you want to be a whale trainer, you have to do your homework, like the Orca Girl said."

After a shy little girl was too tongued-tied to speak, a middle-aged woman with purple spiky hair and piercings galore approached me. I said, half-joking, "Do you have an orca you want Orca Girl to sign?" I winked and said, "Perhaps an orca tattoo?"

She said, "No, but you have some orcas I want you to release."

I snickered, thinking she was ribbing me.

"I'm Nora. You really love these orcas. It's evident to anyone who watches your performances."

"I'm glad it comes across."

"The most loving thing you could do for them is release them from captivity. How would you feel if you were trapped in a bathtub?"

Ah, the bathtub argument. We had been warned about PETA types and had learned how to deal with them in role plays. "Listen, I respect your work and your efforts to protect animals. I can assure you that our orcas are treated with the utmost care."

"It doesn't matter. Orcas in captivity are tortured orcas. An orca can travel one-hundred nautical miles a day, and to put them in a pool where they swim around in circles takes a toll on their brains."

Although I knew I should stick to the script, I wanted to convince her that our orcas were cared for. "Keiko has fathered fifteen calves in captivity. How miserable could he be?"

"There's nothing you can give a wild animal in captivity that he needs."

"Listen, I need to get back to work. Please let our PR department know about your concerns."

"But they don't care the way you do."

I dashed away from the PETA girl, grabbing a bucket of fish for Keiko, Willy, and Milly. If she prattled on, I had no idea what she said. I reassured myself that these orcas had it good. We fed, played with, and nurtured them. They seemed playful and content.

Or maybe that was just me.

Then something struck me. I'm not sure why I had never thought about it before. Perhaps my ecstasy had upstaged all other considerations. These orcas were silent. Dead silent. Was it because they had everything they needed—food, protection, company—so there was no need to communicate about incoming threats, food sources, or their position in the sea?

I was prepping for my next show when Jerry called an emergency staff meeting. I had no idea what could be such an urgent situation that he would interfere with show prep. We gathered in the trainers' room, me in my black-and-white orca wetsuit, itching to get out and play.

"There's no reason to be alarmed, because what I'm going to tell you is an aberration. A trainer has been seriously injured by an orca in Orlando. He was rehearsing when the orca trapped him and held him under. This orca has been known to act out on occasion. There is, most certainly, something wrong with him. The team has him under observation to see if they can uncover any sort of basis for his behavior. They've removed him from performances indefinitely.

"This is going to spread like wildfire among media outlets. It may affect audience numbers and will incite save-the-whales types. The media will swarm for a few days and then forget about us. The American public has a fast and furious attention span that fizzles out when the next scandal hits. For our sake, let's hope it breaks soon. If you should get cornered by someone from the media or animal rights groups, don't stray from the scripts. Excuse yourself as soon as possible."

I scanned the faces in the huddle. Each trainer had terror in their eyes. Oddly, I didn't feel the least bit apprehensive about hitting the pool and rehearsing for our upcoming four performances.

Jerry continued, "If you have any questions or concerns, please feel free to voice them now."

The newest trainer asked, "Are there early warning signs we should look for?"

"As discussed in your training, you should socialize poolside with the animals before jumping into the water. Remember the checklist you received. If the orcas are exhibiting any of those behaviors, do not get in the pool and promptly notify one of the lead trainers."

"A few days ago Chelsea had a close call with Keiko," said Parker.

I shot Parker a shut-the-fuck-up glance that he didn't see.

"Is that true? Why didn't you let me know?" Jerry asked. All eyes were on me.

"Because it was no big deal. He was confused and didn't know I was down there."

"No. He was definitely acting out. It was unmistakable," said Parker glaring at me.

"We're required by law to document this behavior. You need to take this seriously. If there's a pattern of acting out, we will have to pull him from the shows."

"It was a one-time deal. Really. I know Keiko."

I was eager to play with my orca friends and annoyed by the delay. Water park incidents, media, and animal rights folks were becoming increasingly meddlesome and interfering with my passion. These creatures were my family. "Jer, the show must go on. We're on in less than an hour," I blurted, thinking he would be impressed with my pre-performance focus.

Everyone was rapt as Jerry peered at me over his half-glasses. "I don't think you understand. If these incidents aren't handled correctly, Ocean World will cease to exist. There's a movement afoot, spearheaded by PETA, supported by influential celebs, to see to it that we close our doors forever. I'm not being an alarmist when I say we're fighting a losing battle."

"But if they're wrong and these are isolated incidents, what's the problem?" I asked.

"There isn't one, but meddling types love to see problems where there aren't any to further their cause. Orcas provide dramatic footage for their propaganda. There are lots of animal rights groups that exploit a tragedy like this to try to advance their agendas and get publicity."

"Gotcha. I'll make sure to report it next time, if there is a next time."

Tripper and I were at home on a Sunday evening, my one day off, when he hovered over my lounge chair like a low-flying plane with the *Sunday Times* on his laptop, showing me an article about the injury of the trainer in Orlando. A photo of the PETA woman popped out at me.

"She's the one who stopped me after one of my performances."

"You're kidding."

"Why?"

"Don't you know who she is?"

"She's somebody?"

"Yeah, just a super famous grunge singer from Seattle. Her name's Nora Gale."

"To me, she's just a whale of a whiner."

"She says, 'It was only a matter of time before something like this would happen. It was a very angry, very frustrated orca who snapped and decided to take it out on a person. This won't be the last incident of its kind.'"

"They have no frigging idea why orcas do that. Maybe they think we're food or something." The minute I said that, I knew that was the wrong tack. My problem of speaking before thinking always got me in trouble with cautious Tripper.

"Do you really want to be swimming with an animal that sees you as food?"

"God, stop. I have a special bond with them. They know I'm not food."

"Until they think you are."

It was on the tip of my tongue. I was so tempted to reveal my true nature, but the one time I had was disastrous. In a tipsy state, I told a drinking buddy about my whale-ness. She held up her finger and pointed it in my face each time she said the word "whale." "You're a whale? You, Chelsea, are a whale? You're telling me you're a god-damned whale? Yeah, and I'm the fucking Loch Ness monster." Her Loch Ness imitation looked more like the devil on steroids than an underwater sea creature.

Instead of telling Tripper the truth, I said, "I'm not going to have this conversation anymore. Trust me on this."

Ignoring my pleas, he continued, "PETA recommends doing the performances with robots instead of whales. It's safer for the trainers, better for the orcas, and allows the parks to stay open without controversy."

"You're missing the point. What makes this special is the human-orca bond. What kind of bond would I have with robots? What sort of magic would we project to audiences, children especially? They want to experience the wonder and majesty of the orcas first-hand."

"At least robots wouldn't see you as food." Then he said, "Will you watch something?" He set his computer on my lap and played a clip of the last few shows he had attended. Then he played a video of orcas in the wild.

"Yeah, so?"

"What did you notice?"

"Orcas confined versus orcas in the wild. I get it."

"I don't think you do." He displayed the Ocean World clip again and paused it. "Notice the collapsed dorsal fins? That's a sign of distress."

"I thought they always looked like that."

"No, it's atrophy from being confined."

I shoved the computer away. "Geez. Are you trying to take away the most important thing in my life?" I realized too late that I had put orcas before him. "After you."

"I know you love what you do. And I also know you love the orcas. You may have to face the fact that they're mutually exclusive. Perhaps you can serve orcas better by becoming a marine biologist and studying them in the wild."

"They love being in the water with me. I know that for a fact. They're not in distress; it's like we're all one orca pod."

"Only pods don't exist in captivity."

I was torn between bolting upstairs and coming clean. *Don't blow your cover.*

"If you must know, I speak orca. Okay? So I know everything is fine. More than fine—fabulous." I didn't wait for his response. I ran up to bed, switched off the light, and

158

threw the covers over my head, my pounding heart giving way to tears. I may have said too much, but I still hadn't told him the secret that no one else would ever know as long as I lived.

My soggy pillow cradled my head. The dampness was comforting and lulled me to sleep.

Before dawn, I slipped out while Trip was sleeping. I didn't want to face his inquisition to determine whether I had gone off the deep end. I was ready to investigate the orcas' so-called distress signals. I would prove them all wrong.

I toured the tanks as a scientist, rather than a girl in love, and examined Keiko, Milly, and Willy. Indeed, dorsal fin collapse was present in all of them. But maybe it was just a coincidence. Maybe some orcas had it and others didn't. If I was truly a whale, wouldn't I detect distress signals? If my happiness contributed to orca distress, how could I be one? If they were my kind, wouldn't our distress be collective? I felt nothing but unbridled joy when with my orcas.

Could I be another human who used animals for my own amusement while projecting my own happiness onto them? Holding onto the collapsed dorsal fin, I was propelled like a torpedo; balancing on the nose and bounding off—

soaring through the air, I was a flying fish. But the truth may have been the orcas were trying to shake me off.

Perhaps I wasn't picking up on orca communication—distressed or otherwise—because the orcas in captivity had stopped socializing. Wrapped up in my own ecstasy, I never noticed their anguished silence.

I arrive at Ocean World before dawn. My plan is to swim with Keiko an hour before everyone is scheduled to arrive, which I'm not supposed to do, but sometimes you just have to ignore the protocols and take care of yourself. Plus, when you're a whale among whales, human rules don't apply.

When I release Keiko from the holding tank, he torpedoes through the approach canal and into the main pool. He seems frisky if not a bit agitated. I sling a bucket of fish into his gaping pink mouth and jump in next to him. The water is chilly even through my protective layer of neoprene. The chlorine is extra strong today, burning my nostrils.

I climb onto his back and try to stand up and surf, but have to straddle him and hang on for dear life. He's whipping his fluke in a wild rodeo ride effect, sloshing the pool water onto the deck. Whoa! This is insane. I'll stay on until he calms down and soothe him with some pats and rubs.

After he appears to have mellowed, I pop up into a surfing stance and ride him for a few minutes. I flip off, blithely diving behind him; then clutch his tail and catch the currents created by the up-down motion. I release my hold and when Keiko spyhops with his nose out of the water, I grip his pectoral flippers in a ballroom dance position. He spins me around at a dizzying pace, and I lean my head back in glee.

Together we dive thirty-seven feet down. My ears pop as we're plunging. Keiko swiftly reverses his direction, pushes up against my feet, and propels me out of the water in a high-flying swan dive. Then on cue, we circle back to one another and I'm back on top. On Keiko, I'm not a rider, but another fin. We dip and surface, plunge and emerge; it's a game to see how long I can stay upright.

I lose my footing and slip off beneath Keiko. I'll just swim to the surface and jump back on. But I can't. Keiko's blocking my way. I need him to stop thrashing around so I can see my path to the surface. Churning bubbles and writhing bulk obscure my view. I furiously flutter-kick to the right, then to the left, all the while feeling like my lungs are on the verge of exploding. There's no way around. *Move. Seriously. Move!*

Stay calm and be smart about this. Panicking won't help and will use up oxygen. Oh my god. *Get the fuck out of the way!*

When I scream, it comes out in gurgles and bubbles. I need
air. I just have to find a way around, but he's holding me
down. I can't breathe. I swallow to stop the burning sensation
in my throat. My lungs sear. I feel heavy, a weight on top of
me, my limbs paralyzed. There's no way around him. Help
me! Someone, anyone, help! I'm going to die down here.

We're adrift in a pond of phosphorescence. Keiko whistles
and squeaks, moans and trills, filling the pond with
unanswered echolocation. He's singing his freedom, but he is
lost, not remembering the way back to the sea. He says
freedom means nothing if you don't know the way home.
With Keiko, I am home.

Aquamarine Lilli pads adorn the water's surface. Winged
frogs soar and ginger sea turtles with spinnakers billow
around us; the breeze has a sweet citrusy scent. Rain flutters
in cherry blossoms, streaking the water in broad brush
strokes; red petals floating, buoyant candles illuminating the
water's surface. The glistening blooms form a pattern leading
away from the pond. Although I could stay here forever with
Keiko, the currents sweep us into a kaleidoscope canal that
spills us into the sky. Only it's not the sky. We're floating
among waves like striated clouds; the air is water and the
water air. I have a blowhole and he has lungs and he breathes

for me, and I for him. I recognize where we are: I don't want to be here and yet I must. I always knew this day would come—the day our duet would end.

It's the sea, Keiko. Finally the sea.

At first I thought it was heaven, because everything was shiny and white with Christ light slanting through the windows, my vision hazy. The only things missing were the chorus of angels and their bearded boss. And the gates. There were no pearly gates. Thank god, because Lord knows I'm not heaven-ready.

Then I became aware of a pressure in my forearm. An IV. Then the incessant beeping of a heart monitor. I opened my eyes to six pairs of eyes looking down at me, like I was an attraction.

Then I remembered. Keiko. The struggle. To surface. The panic. To breathe. The burning. To live. The heaviness. *But I'm still here! I'm really still here.* I cupped my cheeks to make sure. Yep, flesh and blood Chelsea, not some see-through sparkly angelic version with attached wings. I wanted to leap out of bed and hug my hubby, Parker, and all the other onlookers to celebrate my still-here-ness, but I was attached to too many machines monitoring my vitals.

"Chel, how're you feeling?" Parker asked.

"I guess I made it—huh?" I held my hands out as if to say "Ta-da! Magic!" But in a hospital gown, looking magical is hard to pull off.

"I'll say," said Jerry. "You gave us a scare, but we always knew you were a champ."

"When they found you, you were unconscious at the bottom of the pool. The EMTs pronounced you dead. And then, then you came to. It was un-fucking-believable," said Parker.

"Oh my god. I died?" It was overwhelming to process. Back from the dead. Epically trippy. Easy to say when you're alive and kicking. Not so easy when you've gone the other way.

"What was it like? I mean, did you see a tunnel and white light and stuff?" asked one of the trainers.

"No, nothing like that." I didn't tell them what I did see.

"You'll be glad to hear Keiko has been banned from all future performances and will now just be used as a stud," said Jerry.

I didn't know how to respond. If it meant Keiko would be trapped in a water-cell for the rest of his life and just brought out for forced mating sessions, it made me despondent. "It's not his fault. He didn't mean to hurt me."

I swear they all looked at me like the prescription drugs were talking.

The nurses had okayed a half glass of champagne and a piece of chocolate cake for the occasion. I snuck more champagne from Tripper's glass. I mean, coming back from the dead warrants free-flowing bubbly. Don't you think? Enough with the puritanical restrictions. If I didn't kick the bucket when I officially drowned, surely a bottle of bubbly wasn't going to kill me.

The surviving-a-near-death party replete with balloons, streamers, death shrine-y photos of me, which I could've done without, had ended, not because anyone wanted to leave—after all who doesn't love a hospital party—but because the nurses had said I needed some down time. Me? Are you kidding me? Apparently they hadn't received the memo on Chelsea the Orca Girl. But, okay, I did come back from the dead, so I suppose a little resting wasn't a bad idea.

Tripper Velcroed himself to me, like if he were to unVelcro himself, I might do something else reckless and, this time, not return from the dead. Nervous Nelly had now turned into Terrified Ted. And, of course, I was to blame. Well, I and an orca who was being punished.

I lay in my super-cool adjustable bed, playing with the controls, feeling antsy and restless. So I survived the near-death thing; now can I get on with my life? Tripper was inches from me, his nose buried in the *Wall Street Journal*. He had taken some time off from work to sit vigil, which was sweet, but so unnecessary. I had a team of people checking on me constantly, as if because I had come so close to death, I might slip back there if they didn't monitor me 23/7, allowing one hour of alone time for their cig breaks.

"Hey Tripper."

"Huh?"

"Please hand me my cell."

"Who're you calling? I'll make the call for you. You should rest."

"Thanks, but I need to do this." I honestly never in a million years thought I would make this call, but now that the time had come, my fingers were spry, both in googling her number and in dialing.

"Hi. Is this Nora Gale? It's Chelsea from Ocean World. Do you remember me? We met after one of my performances."

"Of course."

"I might be able to help you."

"A change of heart—huh?"

"Something like that."

Treemail

In hindsight, I think the donuts were a ploy. The red, white, and blue sprinkled donuts, the chocolate-covered cream puffs, and the pink glazed beauties in a box so mesmerized me that I tuned out the drone of the executive team. Just as I snatched a pink one and sunk my teeth into its luscious glaze, the Director interrupted my donut reverie. "Sound good, Riley?" said Fiona. I nodded, having no idea what I had agreed to; best to go with a nod rather than a shake or a shrug in our team meetings.

"Fab," said Fiona. When Fiona said "fab," someone got screwed.

Immediately following the meeting, I burst into my friend Ireland's office and slammed the door. "How'd she screw me? Don't sugarcoat it." I braced for the worst, which would be any assignment requiring me to feign civility.

"You, my friend, are Parks and Forestry's new Arborist Liaison." She emphasized the word "liaison" with exuberant French flair and flashy jazz hands.

I slid down the wall and slumped onto the floor, fiddling with my key necklace. "I can't. I just can't. You have to help me get out of this." Trees were my profession because I was no good at humans.

"Think about it this way: They cancel each other out," said Ireland. "Trees plus people equal…"

"Riley's resignation."

Ireland's mouth wilted into a pout. "You can't leave me alone with bureaucrats and trees." Then she began to scheme, a skill she claimed to have cultivated as a stripper. "Give it a few months. If the awful still outweighs the awesome, we'll quit. Then we'll become digital nomads in an Airstream trailer. Just you and me on the open road. I'll write a book, *Travels With Riley.*"

"And how will we finance our glorified trailer park life before your book becomes a bestseller?"

"We'll get a tree grant with your creds. You're an arborist after all," said Ireland.

"Not anymore. Remember? I'm an Arborist Liaison." I choked out the words.

Did "liaise" necessarily mean face-to-face, or could it mean interaction at arm's length? I felt it would unleash a particularly unpleasant side of human nature. Any time humans were given an open forum, the feedback always devolved into barbs and insults. People would demand that trees be cut, hacked, trimmed, moved, removed, planted, watered, and fertilized on command and claim that trees were hazardous to humans. What about humans being hazardous to trees?

Seattle Parks and Forestry was housed in a state-of-the-art, zero-waste, solar and wind-powered building. Mission alignment: check. The managers urged us to practice what we preached—reduce, reuse, recycle. Spending ten million dollars of taxpayer money on a green facility seemed like a waste, but who was I to judge? I lived in a tiny bamboo house (no trees were sacrificed) on a 500-square-foot plot by a trickling creek that wanted to be a mighty river. My office was five times the size of my home. When I couldn't cut meddlers off at the pass, they'd say, "I could never live in a tiny house." "How can you stand it?" "Doesn't it get claustrophobic?" I stopped volunteering my home's dimensions to thwart cabin fever inquisitions.

Some said it was too bad I was anti-social. If the Committee of Cute assigned you a cuteness designation, they'd claim it was a damned shame you were a hermit.

Apparently, it was acceptable to waste ugliness, but cuteness came with obligations. I tried to stamp out the cute by butchering my red hair into a pixie with mullet tendencies, wearing oversized thrift store clothes, and hiding behind fake clunky glasses (my eyesight was 20-20). I wanted to become excessively inked and pierced to promote standoffishness, but Parks and Forestry mandated we appear wholesome and approachable—grown-up Girl Scouts without beanies and badges. That was just it. I didn't want anyone approaching me unless absolutely necessary, like if I required CPR after tumbling out of a tree. And even then, I wouldn't want to pay the price of being saved—getting up close and personal with another human.

I wasn't always like this.

One summer night when the wind howled, my mom left home to get taco kits, the kind with the self-balancing taco shells. Our family played Last Taco Standing. We loaded our tacos with as much meat, cheese, tomatoes, guacamole, lettuce, and salsa as possible in a battle for the most fully loaded taco still standing. My mom, with a distinct advantage as the resident culinary expert, was the reigning taco champ. The winner was served a deluxe banana split prepared by the losers—banana drenched in butterscotch and covered in coconut and a tower of whipped cream.

While waiting for my mom and strategizing how to grab the taco title from her, I fiddled with the Ninja Turtle Band-Aid on my skinned knee from a wipe-out playing sixth-grade soccer, then picked at my scab until it bled and dripped on the beige carpet. I smudged the drop with my toe; it was the sort of microscopic stain a mother would spot right away.

But no one ever noticed. My mom never came home.

At first, my father and I speculated she had taken a wrong turn, a lame-brained explanation given that she had driven to the store thousands of times. After months of false leads and dead ends, our family resorted to devising our own explanations. My 11-year-old theory was the wind had carried her away to a place where mothers didn't need children. Whenever the wind roared, I imagined it might blow her back to us.

She left no clues as to why she would leave us to fend for ourselves. Believe me, I searched, but I only found a note in fancy cursive imploring my dad to take care of the neglected yard. My childish mind figured that someone had better tend to the yard or my dad might leave, too. I saved my mom's note in a purple lock box and wore the key around my neck. When I missed her, I would insert the tiny key into the hole, unlock the box, and pull out the letter. Her exuberant cursive gave me hope, especially her signature, Savannah.

I became the yard and tree girl, taking such good care of the trees that my dad eventually invested in arborist supplies. I spent evenings and weekends up in the trees, trimming, pruning, and watching the stars bloom in the night. When I was hooked in with tree climbing gear, I fell asleep, an offering to the sky. The first time that happened, my dad, knowing that loved ones vanished, had the whole town on high alert. When I climbed down and nonchalantly strode into the house for a strawberry-lemonade slushy and gingersnaps, my dad laid into me. After his panic subsided, he asked if I wanted a treehouse so we could make my overnights official and safe, for god's sake. I did, in theory, but driving nails into a tree's trunk and branches would wound it. I channeled all my feelings toward trees. Humans, despite their best intentions, always disappointed you. Trees were ever-present, steadfast and, because they were rooted, never walked out of your life.

Ireland was the only human I could abide. As India the stripper, she had become disillusioned with the human race—with men because their penis was their palace, and with women because they shrunk themselves for penis palaces.

Ireland's plan was to dance men's money out of their wallets until she had collected enough to move to Cornwall. As India, a nearly microscopic tick burrowed in her derriere on a New England camping trip and changed the course of her life. She became Ireland, who was once India, stuck in Seattle and unable to move to Cornwall.

India was exotic dance; Ireland was parks and forestry. As India, she stockpiled cash from horny business travelers whose marital rules didn't apply while on the road. While learning to live with Lyme disease, she taught herself to code and traded poles for web-mastering.

Aside from Ireland, I didn't trust insects or humans. They'd both sting, bite, spread disease, or buzz you until you went mad. From Bagworms to Emerald Ash Borers, they even burrowed in trees and caused myriads of problems. Humans interfered where they shouldn't too. Meddlers, Dominators, Parasites, Leeches, and Manipulators burrowed in fellow humans, causing heartache, rage, trauma, despair, even death. If given the choice, I'd take a tree burrower over a human one any day.

During my first week as Arborist Liaison, I brainstormed ways to avoid face-to-face interactions with the public. My best idea: Establish tree emails under Seattle Parks and Forestry's purview. Ireland glared at me when I bounded into her office to tell her we (meaning she) were assigning emails to trees. "You're kidding." I stared back so she knew I wasn't. "How many are we talking?"

"50,000, give or take."

She shot me a wide-eyed glance, screwed up her mouth, and gave me the finger, lovingly. Ireland was all eyes and no face. If I ever needed to, I could draw her in five seconds flat—hangwoman with eyes too big for her body.

Ireland figured out a way to automatically generate 50,000 treemail addresses. "Good thing I found a shortcut; otherwise I'd hang you from a tree by your toenails." She flinched, knowing her words would sting. "Oh, Riley. I'm sorry. When I open my mouth, words sometimes fly out without my consent." I waved it away, not going where she shouldn't have. "Anyway, like anyone cares enough to send a tree an email. Good thing. Who would respond to the complaints?" said Ireland.

"The tree fairy." I posed like a tree, my arms branched skyward, and then flitted around her office, although my wing flapping was more fruit bat than tree fairy.

"You're whacked."

I couldn't deny it. What I did for thrills brought fear and trembling to most. My plot of land, bought with money from my dad's estate, had a stand of Douglas firs that topped 250 feet. In my free time, I was up in the trees as high as I could go without breaking the spindly branches and plunging to my

untimely death or being gorged by a prickly limb. Then I
stretched out on a sturdy limb like a reclining cougar. From
my bird's eye view, I could see the Cascades stretching to the
Pacific and the sprawling expanse of Seattle—the crush of
pleasure-seeking humans clamoring for love and money.
Most mothers would be horrified by such a pastime, and my
mom would have been too, if anyone knew where she was.
That was one advantage of a missing mom; you could do any
reckless thing your heart desired. No one was tasked with
keeping you alive. Except for you. That was my best guess as
to why people didn't hang out in treetops; they had mothers
to intervene in their folly.

Most people didn't realize trees have feelings. They may
be anchored and motionless, except when the wind shakes
them, but they are sentient. So, I knew without a doubt that
my treehouse tree grieved when my dad hung himself from
its branches. I couldn't help but think if I had built a
treehouse, my dad would still be alive. He would've hesitated
to use my tree home as his method of suicide.

I couldn't go near the tree for the longest time. I seethed
and heaved against my dearest and sometimes only friend,
cursing its very existence. I even plotted a chainsaw massacre.
Then a few months after my dad had threaded himself to the
tree, it contracted blight. My fury turned to my deceased
father for using my defenseless treehouse tree as an

accomplice. I begged for forgiveness, plagued with guilt that placing blame had contributed to its disease. I coddled, nursed, and caressed the tree, but the blight won. I had no choice but to chop it down. I hauled the wood in my Dad's pickup to an opening in the forest and built a bonfire. I sprinkled my dad's ashes on the fire. Burning ashes sounds redundant, but Dad didn't want to be sprinkled at sea, adrift for eternity. The sparks flew up and blinked out. I imagined that, in the space between the sparks' glow and the darkness, my dad felt no pain.

My dad's death sent me into a spiral of despair, but ultimately, I couldn't blame him. Unlike my mom, he left behind a recorded song with elucidating lyrics so I wouldn't go crazy searching for clues. He said he could no longer live with a heart so broken; a heart that had never healed after my mom vanished. Sometimes wounds grew as gaping as boundless space, and you fell into eternity's chasm.

I felt cheated by life. The only safe place for me was cradled in branches, obscured by leaves, on the lookout for incoming danger. And on the lookout for her. My mom was still out there somewhere, and, if she emerged, I wanted to be the first to see her.

The first emails that trickled in from concerned citizens of
Seattle were as expected: cut the white birch tree, trim the
dogwood, move the sweet gum from our view. I was the
glorified complaint department. But then something
happened one morning after I had spent the night in a
Douglas, a little breezy, but otherwise glorious. And, oh the
sunrise, from a bird's eye view—I saw why birds are so
chirpy.

I opened an email to Elm Tree 5839.

Dear Mr. Elm,

I'm dying. I've decided I want to become you for eternal
life. I want my ashes buried by your roots so I can nourish
you. Your branches would become my arms, your leaves my
hair, and your stature the height of my dreams. I could watch
as the world unfolds, sensing the sun's warmth on our
branches and our leaves sprouting in the spring.

Best regards,

Bertram

Then this one to Fir Tree 9368.

Dear Miss Fir,

Don't tell anyone, but I have no friends. You are my one
and only. When I'm hurting, I sit beneath you. Your presence

stills my nerves and makes me whole. Before I go, I hold you until I feel your spirit take root in mine.

Respectfully,

Rebecca

And this one to Birch Tree 2635.

Dear Mr. Birch,

I lost my baby girl, Bailey, alive for just five days; her remains are in a pine box, and I would like to bury her beneath you. I want her to see the sky through your branches, to admire your bark shimmering with the fading sun.

Yours truly,

Lena

As this continued for weeks, I felt increasingly cornered by humans and their bottomless angst. I kept reading. The weight of the human condition crushed my chest, like a tree had collapsed on top of me. Their troubles threatened my carefully crafted reality. After my dad died, I sealed off my heart—safe from those who would be careless with it, safe from those who could disappear without a trace.

I rushed into Ireland's office, feeling slightly dizzy and holding my tingling face. She was hunched over her keyboard, all shoulder bones, elbows, and limbs—a graceful praying mantis.

"I don't get what's happening," I said, trying to catch my breath.

"With what?" She swiveled around.

"The emails." I paced in her barren Zen office with exactly one rock sculpture.

"Getting barraged?" Her eyes followed me. I nodded. "What a pain in the ass."

"Where's your chair?"

"Chucked it. People were lingering. I knew you'd become the complaint department."

"That's just it. They're mostly not complaints."

"They're not?"

"Just the opposite—more like, I don't know, love letters." I cringed as I said the words aloud.

"Ha!" She pointed at me. "I knew you had secret admirers."

"Except they're not for me. They're love letters to trees."

"Huh?" She spun her chair around. When she completed her 360, she said, "What are you going to do?"

"I don't know. I've created a monster. I can't do this."

"Why don't you just answer them?"

"God, no."

"Why the hell not?"

"What do I know about soothing troubled souls?"

"But you know trees—right?"

"Yeah, so?"

"Answer as though you're the trees."

No way in hell. Not now, not ever. I made up an excuse to leave Ireland's office as quickly as possible, left the office mid-day, and did the only thing that made sense. I climbed my Douglas fir for thirty minutes up to the spindliest branches. I had never been that high and, judging from the too frequent cracks under my feet, I willed myself to stop before it was too late. From my perch, none of the pain and agony of being human was visible. Perhaps I would never come down again. I tried to tune out the clutching neediness and desperation of the emailers. Their lives weren't mine to fix. Some lives were destined to be broken.

I eventually came down off my perch and returned to work, all the while plotting my escape—one that didn't include Ireland, an Airstream, or digital nomadism. My dream job: a ranger in the remotest wilderness of Alaska, accessible only by seaplane or boat and a week of backpacking. The U.S. Park Service would drop provisions once a month, and I would live out my days on the Katmai Peninsula with the brown bears.

One day while researching positions with the U.S.P.S., I noticed an email in my inbox addressed to Ms. Maple 5461. Since maples were my favorite tree, I clicked on it.

Dear Ms. Maple,

You remind me of my daughter lost long ago—so bold and beautiful in all seasons. I wasn't able to watch her grow into the incredible woman she has become. I had to leave for reasons she will never understand. She hasn't seen me since the wind carried me away. Will you be our meeting place tonight at 9:00?

Savannah

My heart clung to what my eyes wouldn't believe. *Was it really her? How had she found me? Why was she contacting me this way?* My more rational thought was that someone was playing a practical joke, but who could be so cruel? The broken child part of me wanted to believe that she had resurfaced. I would go to the maple.

I didn't complete a lick of work after that. I wanted to knock myself out and wake up right before my meeting at the maple. I reread the email for hours looking for new clues and talked myself in and out of going a dozen times. *If it was her, what if she was a no-show? Would I have anything to say to her? What if she wasn't who I remembered? What if she showed up only to break my heart again? Would she be proud of the person I had become?*

I couldn't stop watching the clock. In a frenzy, I unplugged the clock and hid the one on my computer. I wanted to tell Ireland, but feared she would think I had totally lost it. At some point Ireland tapped on my closed office door and I waved her away, pretending to be on a call.

Night finally arrived and I hit the ladies' room. In the mirror was someone I had never seen before. Before this moment, I had stopped caring. Now I fussed with my hair and removed my glasses. I even painted my lips for the first time in ages. *Silly, she won't see your lipstick in the dark.* I didn't feel ready. I mussed and fussed some more, spiking my hair, flattening it, pushing it into and out of my face. I struck poses that conveyed sophistication, wisdom, worldliness, and healthy detachment. But through them all, I could see the scared little girl I still was. I realized I'd never feel ready, so I coaxed myself out the door.

My first move was to the maple. I considered climbing it and surprising her from above. But she never knew my tree-climbing self, so that might seem odd, especially for a grown woman. Who knew? Maybe she liked whimsy and playfulness. But more likely she preferred a grounded, practical approach. Of course, leaving one's child was straight-up heartless, not practical, or whimsical. But I didn't want to greet her with bitterness. It wasn't (so much) that I harbored resentment over her disappearing act; I experienced emptiness where a mother should have been. I decided to hide behind an adjacent cedar—a scaredy-cat move—so I could see her before she saw me and escape if it felt too weird. At 9:00 I peered around the cedar. The silhouette of a woman approached the maple. I felt my driving pulse all the way to my fingers and toes. An acidic taste surfaced in my throat, like I might lose the curried chicken frozen dinner I had forced down. I held myself so I wouldn't fly apart and scatter into little pieces.

My mom looked terribly gaunt. Perhaps she wasn't well. Maybe the grief of leaving us had eaten away at her. The first thing I'd do was feed her—a banana split, her favorite. Then I'd tell her all about the years she missed, leaving out the Dad part.

When the woman came into focus, she wasn't the she I expected. I bolted out from behind the cedar to run interference. "Ireland, what are you doing here? Listen, you can't stay. I'm waiting for someone, a private meeting."

Ireland bit her lip and gazed up at the maple, then at me, then at the maple. She seemed agitated, like she wanted to say something but couldn't find the words.

"I'll fill you in later. Promise," I said.

Ireland spoke haltingly. "There's a tree that reminds me of my daughter lost so long ago—so bold and beautiful. She hasn't seen me since the wind swept me away from her. I want to go home to her."

"No! Don't do this to me." What was left of my heart broke off into my churning stomach. "You're so fucking cruel." I twisted away.

She moved in closer and touched my arm. "But don't you see?"

I shook off her hand. "I don't see anything except for a heartless person who I thought was my best friend. How could you do this to me?"

"Hope is alive in your heart, which makes you…"

"Nothing but a fucking fool."

"You claim to be jaded, but how many would hold onto hope for so long?"

"Whatever, India." I wanted the stripper name to bite. I flung the letter and sprinted away from her, the maple, the park, and through the neighborhoods, by the bay, until my lungs burned and my legs gave out. I fell forward, my tears mixing with the dewy grass, my body held by the earth, my heart bleeding into the ground.

I had gone against my one rule: Never trust a human. Ireland's charade showed me a desperate soul who should let go and move on. But when your mother doesn't even say goodbye, how could she not be out there somewhere?

The night was a blur of cars, Victorian facades, contemporary urban condos, ranch homes, dog parks, and playgrounds. Rain fell, drenching and chilling me beyond caring. I hoped to contract pneumonia and perish—another casualty of the soggy streets. I couldn't face my boss, the tree emails, and especially not Ireland. The pain of being made a fool seared like wildfire, but as the flames faded to embers, a sixth grader with a skinned knee appeared in the dimming light, clutching the curly cursive letter. Then a grown woman teetering in the treetops, risking life and limb to see, to really see, when all I needed to see was this: My mother was gone, but I didn't have to be.

As dawn streaked the sky ginger peach and illuminated silhouettes of homes clinging to the park's perimeter, I huddled at the foot of a knobby ancient elm and drafted a letter in my head. Roving gangs of homeless people with soiled backpacks and scruffy dogs shared nods of recognition. I popped up and retraced my steps through the neighborhoods into the office, keeping a low profile—me, the drowned rat. I typed and printed the letter and raced into Ireland's office.

She eyed me up and down. "Geez, what happened to you?"

"Listen…"

"Oh, Riley, I was a complete moron. I don't know what I was thinking. I guess I wanted you to see that your mother would be so proud of who you've become. And I want you to stop…" She hesitated and glanced down at her hands. "But I royally fucked up. Will you ever forgive me?" She avoided my gaze, her head and shoulders drooping under the weight of her assumed guilt.

"Are you kidding me? It was a stroke of genius."

"It was?" Her eyes lit up.

I handed her the letter. "Read this aloud, please."

"Dear Ms. Maple,

I need you to keep watch for someone. I've done so from treetops, but I'm ready to come down from the boughs, to peer at trees from below, trusting that treetops hold secrets I may never know. When your leaves rustle, I'll imagine my mom shaking your branches saying she's out there somewhere. And letting me know I can stop searching.

Love,
Riley"

Ireland's voice tapered to a hoarse murmur; her trembling hands clutched the letter. She scrunched her face to squeeze back the tears. "You don't have to stop looking."

"I know."

She wrapped herself around me, her bony arms like branches. Her heart beat against mine, at first arrhythmically. We clung to each other until our heartbeats synced. I knew then I couldn't sustain myself on trees alone.

"Are you sure you're ready?" Ireland stroked my damp, tangled hair. I nodded. Her owl eyes blinked open. "Should we make it official and bury this thing under the maple?" Her hand flew up, waving the letter above our heads. I grabbed her hand and rushed toward the door. I paused abruptly and yanked the keychain necklace from my neck, cradling it in my palm. "And this too."

The next day, I settled in at my desk with my morning coffee, its aroma intoxicating, and navigated to my email inbox and the countless unanswered emails. Rereading the first few was like seeing them for the first time. I watched as my fingers composed responses, feeling like another's voice flowed through me onto the page—a voice from long ago, a voice connected to someone's heart. I couldn't be sure it was mine, though. It had been so long.

Dear Mr. Bertram,

I know you will make a lovely elm. You have my word we'll bury your ashes beneath me. Best wishes for a peaceful transition. By the way, life as a tree is magnificent; even better than being human.

Warm regards,

Mr. Elm

Dear Rebecca,

Climb in my branches as high as your limbs will take you. You'll feel what it's like to be held by a tree. You can spend an evening with me, watching the twilight fade to black. And when the moon rises, you'll see it alight from the treetops.

All my best,

Miss Fir

Dear Lena,

Come bury your beloved Bailey beneath me. It will give me strength to be a majestic birch. Her song will be etched in the delicate white curls of my bark; her belly-laugh will flutter my leaves. In autumn when my leaves turn brilliant yellow-orange like wind poppies, her spirit will perform pirouettes. Then come and be in my presence. Feel her through me.

Very truly yours,

Miss Birch

Acknowledgements

Z, my lovable geek, did the heavy lifting on editing, self-publishing, web creation, and was the captain of team moral support. Without you, this book would have remained on my hard drive for eternity. Or until an asteroid collided with our planet.

A huge thanks to my writers' group—Laurel, Monica, Gye, Tami, Suzanne, and Susan—for being fierce writing and story craft warriors and for limiting the times you deemed my work "dark" and "quirky," even though you were thinking it. Although just three of us remain, the rest of you are with me as I travel the uncharted path of self-publishing.

Monica gets her own line of gratitude, as she graciously volunteered to work her editing magic on half of these stories. Thanks to Karin and Jody who polished the other half and made them shine.

Christine's perfectly-timed endorsement was so damn good! Many thanks for your title help and for tolerating my writerly inquisitions during family holidays and vacations.

Even though my mom says she doesn't read fiction, and when she does, she doesn't enjoy it, she has read most of my stories. Thanks, Mom, for venturing into a genre that's not your favorite, for your once little scribe who filled scores of journals. We will one day light a giant bonfire.

To my dad who introduced me to the art of the story with his tales of Fred, the mischievous fox, Leo the Lion, Mike the Monkey, who lived in the deciduous forest and tucked us into bed at night. I think I might need to reinstate Fred Fox stories to cure my insomnia.

To Mark, whose ongoing support is invaluable. Working with you has been the honor of a lifetime.

Many thanks to Amy, whose brilliant insights and encouragement make it a joy to write. To Sally Stromer who has diligently read and commented on everything I've ever written. And to Andy, Adam, Eric, and Calle for their friendships and love. For my nephews and niece who delight me with their wisdom, artistry, and athleticism.

Much gratitude to my friends for their unconditional love and support. To Mary who has always shared my heart and walks with me wherever I go. To Libby for exploring the wild side with me. To my book club buddies, many of whom don't like short stories but read mine nonetheless. To my dance ladies, whose blissed-out choreography and comradery infuse me with joy. And to Mike for a perfectly-timed heart transplant. Did you give me yours or did I give you mine?

To Liz and Suzanne, the keepers of my heart and head.

I'm forever grateful to my Uncle Charlie, poet extraordinaire, for his celestial writerly presence and to Ron Billingsley for opening my eyes to magic at just the right time. And for dashing across the cafeteria with news of my final paper for your honors course, *The Future of Spaceship Earth*, and proclaiming that it was a work of beauty.

About the Author

Ann Tinkham is a writer based in Boulder, Colorado. She is an anti-social butterfly, pop-culturalist, virtual philosopher, ecstatic dancer, political and java junkie. When she's not tinkering with words, she's seeking adventures. Ann has talked her way out of an abduction and talked her way into the halls of the United Nations. She hitchhiked up a mountain in Switzerland and worked her way down the corporate ladder. Ann has flown on a trapeze and traded on the black market in Russia. She cycles up steep canyons, hikes to glacial lakes and mountain peaks, and blazes her own ski trails.

Her fiction and essays have appeared in many literary journals, including Foliate Oak, Slow Trains, The Adirondack Review, The Citron Review, The Literary Review, Toasted Cheese, Wild Violet, Word Riot, and others. Ann's essay, "The Tree of Hearts" was nominated for a Pushcart Prize and her story, "Afraid of the Rain" was nominated for Sundress's Best of the Net Anthology.

CPSIA information can be obtained
at www.ICGtesting.com
Printed in the USA
LVHW111515260919
632369LV00004B/693/P